Brian Aldiss was born in Norfolk in During the Second World War he served in the British Army in the Far East. He began his professional career as a bookseller in Oxford and then went on to become Literary Editor of the *Oxford Mail*. For many years Brian Aldiss was a film reviewer and poet. The three outspoken and bestselling novels making up *The Horatio Stubbs Saga* (*The Hand-Reared Boy* (1970), *A Soldier Erect* (1971), and *A Rude Awakening* (1978)) brought his name to the attention of the general book-buying public, but in the science fiction world his reputation as an imaginative and innovative writer had long been established. *Non-Stop*, his first SF novel, was published in 1958, and among his many other books in this genre are *Hothouse* (published in 1962 and winner of the Hugo Award for the year's best novel), *The Dark Light Years* (1964), *Greybeard* (1964) and *Report on Probability A* (1968). In 1965, the title story of *The Saliva Tree*, written as a celebration of the centenary of H. G. Wells, won a Nebula Award. In 1968, Aldiss was voted the United Kingdom's most popular SF writer by the British Science Fiction Association. And in 1970, he was voted 'World's Best Contemporary Science Fiction Author'. Brian Aldiss has also edited a number of anthologies, a picture book on science fiction illustration (*Science Fiction Art* (1975)) and has written a history of science fiction, *Billion Year Spree* (1973). The three volumes of the epic Helliconia trilogy, published to critical acclaim, are *Helliconia Spring* (1982), *Helliconia Summer* (1983) and *Helliconia Winter* (1985).

By the same author

BRIAN ALDISS

Space, Time and Nathaniel

PANTHER
Granada Publishing

Panther Books
Granada Publishing Ltd
8 Grafton Street, London W1X 3LA

Published by Panther Books 1979
Reprinted 1985

First published in Great Britain by
Faber & Faber Ltd 1957

The following stories have appeared variously in the following magazines:
'T', 'Our Kind of Knowledge', 'Psyclops', 'Conviction', 'Criminal
Record', 'The Failed Men', 'There is a Tide', 'Pogsmith', 'Outside' and
'Panel Game' in *Authentic*, *Nebula*, *New Worlds* and *Science-Fantasy*. To
the editors of these magazines I offer my thanks for permission to collect
them here, slightly revised.

To Edmund Crisp for permission to reprint 'Outside' from his *Best sf
Two* (Faber and Faber), and to Messrs Wm. S. Heinemann and *The
Observer* for permission to reprint 'Not For An Age' from *A.D. 2500*, I
also offer thanks.

ISBN 0-586-04989-4

Printed and bound in Great Britain by
Collins, Glasgow

Set in Intertype Times

If, as mine is, thy life a slumber be,
    Seem, when thou readst these lines, to dream of me . . .
If men be worlds, there is in every one
    Some thing to answer in some proportion
All the world's riches: and in good men this
Virtue our form's form and our soul's soul is.

John Donne: *To Mr. R. W.*

Contents

Introduction

STAN (the book is known by its acronym in these regions) was my first science fiction book, so my publishers were cautious: it was a small edition, and copies are now as rare as roubles in Arundel. It was reviewed a bit, here and there, and the reviews were also cautious. I felt at the time that a little more enthusiasm would have been welcome – but science fiction was then regarded with the sort of apprehension normally reserved, in England at least, for big dogs and small children.

Among the reviews were one from the *South Rhodesian Herald* and another from the *Bulawayo Examiner*. They were receptive to science fiction in Bulawayo in those days. I received a fan letter from a man who wrote to me from The Irish Guest House, Bulawayo (one of my favourite addresses, which I later used in a novel, on the principle of 'waste not, want not'.) They have less time for reading nowadays in Bulawayo and in what was Southern Rhodesia. On the whole, that part of the world was a good deal more placid and better farmed than now, a safer place to live in for both black and white.

One of the stories, 'There is a Tide', is set in Africa, and depicts a future when the blacks have taken over the continent. Although readers and critics have often spoken of my work as pessimistic, hindsight shows how optimistic I was, how optimistic we all were. True, there has been a great natural catastrophe in the story, but the black nations of Africa are co-operating to deal with the catastrophe, and behave in a civilized way. In the mid-fifties, we had good hope for emergent nations being given their freedom from colonialism, and anticipated their contributions to world peace.

Africa is not the only exotic place embedded in these fictions. One story begins in Singapore, mentioning a café, *The Iceberg*, where I once used to eat. *The Iceberg* is gone now and no longer are people permitted to be sick into

9

privet hedges, for the anti-litter laws are commendably strict. Singapore is probably the cleanest city in Asia, as well as one of the largest; certainly it is cleaner than London. While London's star has sunk, Singapore's has risen, as the talent for enterprise and trade passes elsewhere. Provision for *that* kind of idea is not made in my story. Strange victories and despairs move below the surface, but I was then too young to appreciate how irreversible are the trends of history.

As perhaps the characteristic tone of these stories indicates, I had learnt the art of short-story writing – or had at least picked up the desire to learn the art – from H. H. Munro, generally known as 'Saki'. I received a collection of his stories as a Christmas present when I was twelve, and read it through and through. The ghosts of Clovis and Reginald still haunt me, not to mention Saki's fine English style.

My stories were composed in my head whilst I was working in a bookshop. They often accumulated phrase by phrase, and paragraph by paragraph were committed to memory. I became, or imagined I became, an able exponent of the paragraph. It was my ambition to read a review which declared roundly, 'Aldiss is our most noted modern exponent of the paragraph.' Even in its peaceful and productive days, Bulawayo was blind to the beauties of my paragraphing. How intimately such unresponsiveness to prose has contributed to the sorry present plight of Rhodesia I must leave to the wise and to Sir George Steiner to determine.

Sometimes the stories were influenced by whatever reading I was surreptitiously doing in the bookshop at the time. Thus, the story 'Supercity', which features Nathaniel, was founded on a genial dislike of André Gide's 'The Fruits of the Earth', which I thought enormously pretentious. There also one Nathaniel is addressed. (If I didn't mention such minutiae, who would ever know?)

'Supercity' is not produced 'Super City'. Much of my art was and has remained mildly deflationary. This story was letting the air out of the tyres of galactic epics, in its small way. But I agree that the title of that story is a bit too much, *and* the title of the collection, which, in those days

10

when Joseph Stalin was dead but not denounced, was far too elusive for the somewhat plodding British sf ethos of the day.

Critics complained that I was too clever. But they missed one melancholy cleverness. One hates to be called too clever by people who can't see how clever one is. My ambition had been to become a poet. Then I encountered real poetry. (When I arrived in Oxford, the fashionable poets were still T. S. Eliot and John Donne). Sf seemed a more likely outlet for a minor talent; since it lacked its Eliots and Donnes, one might therefore pass muster. STAN's contents page was designed in the form of a sonnet, with its octet and sestet, as a sort of In Memoriam to old ambitions.

If I'd really done my homework, it would have scanned and rhymed.

B.W.A.

Oxford 1979

Introduction

What happens to old science fiction? Is it as expendable as last year's calendars?

There's no denying it is disconcerting to read H. G. Wells's *The Shape of Things to Come* today and find that in 1965 the World State became a reality, following the meeting of the nations at Basra – convened, if you please, by the Transport Union. But the sf reader enjoys being disconcerted (indeed, the major part of an sf writer's effort is devoted directly to disconcerting him), and he will regard the Basra affair as something that happened on an alternate time track.

Go further back than Wells, and period charm takes over utterly. Cyrano de Bergerac, writing in the seventeenth century, whizzes up to the sun in a vacuum-powered box that delights by its impossibility, while his arguments on such subjects as why the heat of the sun does not destroy, or why space travellers feel no hunger, are clever, logical, ingenious – and pleasurably crackpot.

Come upon sf written more recently than Wells, and you run up against an excellent range of oddities that happened in some other space-time continuum. In Rex Gordon's *No Man Friday* – to name one of my favourite novels – we find that the first man into space was a forty-four-year-old Scotsman.

I have a suspicion that more than a whiff of period charm hangs over *Space, Time and Nathaniel*, known familiarly by its acronym of Stan. Although it was published only ten years ago, time marches on, and the genre to which these stories belong has changed a great deal. They themselves, I hope I'm not too wrong or immodest in saying, helped bring about that change.

What I was endeavouring to do was write sf that would fit into the established canon. I see now that their style made them slightly different, as did their approach to already stereotyped subjects like space flight. They gave me joy in the writing before I had begun to worry much about the art of fiction; readers may feel in them the sense I had of the freedom of sf as a form. For these were my first stories, and this was my first sf book. It has been out of print for several years, and I am delighted that Four Square has decided to bring it out again.

Fortunately, I never wrote the predictive type of fiction, so that the pages that follow are not cluttered with too many Basras, vacuum-powered boxes, or space-going Scotsmen. All the same, there are oddities like the video record in 'Criminal Record', or the telly future in 'Panel Game'; the generally prevailing mood seems to me markedly to belong to the fifties. It is an indication that – whatever it may pretend to do – sf is essentially a reflection of its own day. I hope readers will not find the mirror too tarnished; alternatively, I hope they will not insist that these are better stories than my later ones!

Oxford, December 1965   *Brian W. Aldiss*

Introduction

The Introduction is often the best part of a book, although I refuse to guarantee that in this case. The reading of introductions is an occupation in its own right; strange nobody has written about it, analysed it, interpreted it 'in the light of present-day knowledge'! Introductions are turned to many purposes; they may be almost as private as summer-houses in country gardens, given over to praise of wifely typing abilities, thanks to helpful librarians, acknowledgments for the loan of deck chairs. Or they may be a more business-like peep behind scenes, a discussion of sources, a monologue on methods. Or – for there are as many varieties of introduction as of book – they may be something else again. This one, for instance, is something else again.

Some of us over thirty remember the days when science fiction was not mentioned in respectable company. Now, it is. Much as we may deplore any company whose only recommendation is its respectability, this change is pleasant. It gives us the feeling that we were Right All Along. Or, if not that, the less droll feeling that comes when the rank outsider we backed romps home into some sort of place.

This change in the status of sf (to call it by its familiar name) has engendered much wild and some wildly interesting argument. Two opposing schools of thought have sprung up, bellowing pros and cons. From the belligerent camps have come uneasy detractors like J. B. Priestley, splendid protagonists like Edmund Crispin. Meanwhile, like stretcher-bearers busy between the two armies, the sf writers themselves continue to write sf. And when their collections of short stories appear, they appear, very properly, with nothing so provoking as an introduction attached. Now, flinging aside my stretcher, I venture an introduction.

Since so many subtle things have been said already in the matter, there remains only the obvious, which may have been overlooked. Sf is a rich field for contention. This glimpse of the undeniable is well worth pursuing, for contention waxes not merely because sf is new – that is, in so far as anything is new; it continues to wax because sf, while apparently a *genre*, which implies conformity to a set pattern or type, is actually too broad a field to stay in any one category. The corsets of conformity pinch on all sides! Although still engagingly young, sf is rapidly becoming capable of embracing as many nuances as what is occasionally, disgustingly, called 'mainstream' literature itself. It is workable, the soil is rich: given the weather, anything will grow.

This is why, despite many attacks upon it, sf continues to flourish. Any attack can only hit one little bit of the target, and whoever knows sf knows this. In its time, sf has been dismissed because it is idle fancy, mere gadgetry, basically unscientific, too scientific, paints too grey a picture, is too highly coloured, is not escapist enough, is just a modern fairy-tale. And the truth? Sometimes it is none of these things; not infrequently it is all of them. As for the remark that much sf content is 'unlikely', surely such factualism requires no answer. *Everything*, if we consider coolly, is unlikely: the stars, the fingernails. Likely and unlikely are the same word.

About four years ago, appearances suggested that sf might turn into a realm for best-sellers. For the first time, clothbound books appeared in this country bearing simultaneously the names of science fiction and hitherto responsible publishers. A boom of some sort was on, and we were all very flustered. The comparatively small number of sf writers was unable to meet the demand; as a result, novels labelled 'science fiction' were produced by authors with no sf traditions behind them. Four cents a word and no questions asked was the order of the day! These new novels, unfortunately, adhered to none of the carefully worked-out rules of the game. Consequently, the public was left with an erroneous – or, perhaps worse, a nebulous – idea of what kind of experience it was being offered by the main school of writers.

Now the 'anything goes' stage is over. It killed itself. The boom became a boomerang. In many ways, the present period is more interesting. (It is, for instance, again possible

15

to read *all* the sf as it is published; whether this is desirable is a question for individual taste.) It seems as if sf will, with occasional exceptions called John Wyndham, appeal only to a minority, like poetry, caviare and Christmas swims in the Serpentine. Like poetry: perhaps that's the best simile, for sf and poetry have much in common. Both have a sly, surprising music; neither are particularly easy to write.

Why poetry attracts so few readers is a matter for sad speculation to poets; as the wit said, poets are born not paid. With sf, the answer is more obvious, although it may apply to poetry too. Each sf story demands something from its reader, even such small constructions as you will find in this book: a reorientation, a willingness to consider a fragment of someone else's Xanadu. This is not exactly comfortable. The circulating libraries are naturally unwilling to subscribe.

My idea of sf as a sort of poetry is, I admit, not a popular one in some sf circles. But as yet space travel, telepathy and the rest of our apparatus is just a dream: and was there ever such a luring dream as space travel? These things are more successfully treated as symbols than as facts. Only a few geniuses like James Blish and Hal Clement are deft enough to stir in the scientific patter convincingly.

This is a self-conscious age: Science, which is man's investigation into his environment and himself, reveals us continually to ourselves, and the more clearly the picture is seen, the more mysterious it is seen to be. There is a thing called 'life', a flame which, like the Olympic fire, is passed from torch to torch, and while we hold it we must examine ourselves by its light. We are, to speak soberly, fantastic. We drive cars, drink Horlicks, peer down microscopes: whatever will we be up to next? That is the question the science-fiction writer perpetually asks; with his super-self-consciousness, he sees the future glancing back mockingly at him dithering by the cross-roads – and he attempts a retaliatory stare.

A criticism of sf that is frequently raised is that it has no real characters. This is as true and as unanswerable as those complaints that a certain piece of music has no real tunes in it. It is a fairly naïve comment, missing the point of the matter, for the main purpose of sf lies elsewhere. The virtue of sf is that it presents man in relation to his surroundings: man on another planet, man in a different era, man faced with alien life, man against one of his own inventions. Without making too large a claim for it, we may say that sf is the only way of dealing with ourselves as an organic part of the universe; whereas the ordinary novel can only portray us as a part of human society. This is the justification of the term *science*-fiction' – not, perhaps, as hideous a term as it seems.

I am aware that this sounds forbidding. So, unclothed, are the skeletons we all carry round with us; yet the actual flesh can be very inviting. And sf, like a growing lad, is developing a sense of humour, which is a healthy sign. Frederic Brown, William Tenn and John Wyndham (not to extend the list) can be first-rate humorists, Margaret St Clair's 'Prott' is a gem of tragi-comedy; and some of the stories included here may be labelled 'funny'. Sf copes with the indignities as well as the dignity of man.

But the two armies mentioned before are still in the field: I must resume my stretcher.

April 1956

SPACE

By the time T was ten years old, his machine was already on the fringes of that galaxy. T was not his name – the laboratory never considered christening him – but it was the symbol on the hull of his machine and it will suffice for a name. And again, it was not his machine; rather, he belonged to it. He could not claim the honourable role of pilot, nor even the humbler one of passenger; he was a chattel whose seconds of utility lay two hundred years ahead.

He lay like a maggot in the heart of an apple at the centre of the machine, as it fled through space and time. He never moved; the impulse to move did not present itself to him, nor would he have been able to obey if it had. For one thing, T had been created legless – his single limb was an arm. For another, the machine hemmed him in on all sides. It nourished him by means of pipes which fed into his body a thin stream of vitamins and proteins. It circulated his blood by a tiny motor that throbbed in the starboard bulkhead like a heart. It removed his waste products by a steady syphoning process. It produced his supply of oxygen. It regulated T so that he neither grew nor wasted. It saw that he would be alive in two hundred years.

T had one reciprocal duty. His ears were filled perpetually with an even droning note and before his lidless eyes there was a screen on which a dull red band travelled for ever down a fixed green line. The drone represented (although not to T) a direction through space, while the red band indicated (although not to T) a direction in time. Occasionally, perhaps only once a decade, the drone changed pitch or the band faltered from its green line. These variations registered in T's consciousness as acute discomforts, and accordingly he would adjust one of the two small wheels by his hand, until conditions returned to normal and the even tenor of monotony was resumed.

Although T was aware of his own life, loneliness was one of the innumerable concepts which his creators arranged he should never sense. He lay passive, in an artificial contentment. His time was divided not by night or day, or waking or sleeping, or by feeding periods, but by silence or speaking. Part of the machine spoke to him at intervals, short monologues on duty and reward, instructions as to the working of a simple apparatus that would be required two centuries ahead. The speaker presented T with a carefully distorted picture of his environs. It made no reference to the inter-galactic night outside, nor to the fast backward seepage of time. The idea of motion was not a factor to trouble an entombed thing like T with. But it did refer to the Koax, and in reverent terms, speaking also – but in words filled with loathing – of that inevitable enemy of the Koax, Man. The machine informed T that he would be responsible for the complete destruction of Man.

T was utterly alone, but the machine which carried him had company on its flight. Eleven other identical machines – each occupied by beings similar to T – bore through the continuum. This continuum was empty and lightless and stood in the same relationship to the universe as a fold in a silk dress stands to the dress; when the sides of the fold touch, a funnel is formed by the surface of the material inside the surface of the dress. Or you may liken it to the negativity of the square root of minus two, which has a positive value. It was a vacuum inside a vacuum. The machines were undetectable, piercing the dark like light itself and sinking through the hovering millennia like stones.

The twelve machines were built for an emergency by a non-human race so ancient that they had abandoned the construction of other machinery aeons ago. They had progressed beyond the need of material assistance – beyond the need of corporeal bodies – beyond the need at last of planets with which to associate their tenuous egos. They had come finally, in their splendid maturity, to call themselves only by the name of their galaxy, Koax. In that safe island of several million stars they moved and had their being, and brooded over the coming end of the universe. But while they brooded, another race, in a galaxy far beyond the meaning of distance, grew to seniority. The new race, unlike the Koax, was extravert and warlike; it tumbled out among the stars like an explosion, and its name was Man. There came a time when this race, spreading from one infinitesimal body, had multiplied, and filled its own galaxy. For a while it paused, as if to catch its breath – the jump between stars is nothing to the gulf between the great star cities – and then the time/space equations were formulated: Man strode to the nearest galaxy armed with the greatest of all weapons, Stasis. The temporal mass/energy relationship that regulates the functioning of the universe, they found, might be upset in certain of the more sparsely starred galaxies by impeding their orbital revolution, causing, virtually, a fixation of the temporal factor – Stasis – whereby everything affected ceases to continue along the universal time-flow and ceases thereupon to exist. But Man had no need to use this devastating weapon, for as on its by-product, the Stasis drive, he swept from one galaxy to another, he found no rival, nor any ally. He seemed destined to be sole occupant of the universe. The innumerable planets revealed only that life was an accident. And then the Koax were reached.

The Koax were aware of Man before he knew of their existence, and their immaterial substance cringed to think that soon it would be torn through by the thundering drives of the Supreme Fleet. They acted quickly. Materializing on to a black dwarf, a group of their finest minds prepared to combat the invader with every power possible. They had some useful abilities, of which being able to alter and decide the course of suns was not the least. And so nova after nova flared into the middle of the Supreme Fleet. But Man came invincibly on, driving into the Koax like a cataclysm. From a small frightened tribe a few hundred strong, roaming a hostile earth, he had swelled into an unquenchable multitude, ruling the stars. But as the Koax wiped out more and more ships, it was decided that their home must be eliminated by Stasis, and ponderous preparations were begun. The forces of Man gathered themselves for a massive final blow.

Unfortunately, a Fleet Library Ship was captured intact by the Koax, and from it something of the long, tangled history of Man was discovered. There was even a plan of the Solar System as it had been when Man first knew it. The Koax heard for the first time of Sol and its attendants. Sol at this time, far across the universe, was a faintly radiating smudge with a diameter twice the size of the planetary system that had long ago girdled it. One by one, as it had expanded into old age, the planets had been swallowed into its bulk; now even Pluto was gone to feed the dying fires. The Koax finally developed a plan that would rid them entirely of their foes. Since they were unable to cope in the present with the inexhaustible resources of Man, they evolved in their devious fashion a method of dealing with him in the far past when he wasn't even there. They built a dozen machines that would slip through time and space and annihilate Earth before Man appeared upon it; the missiles would strike, it was determined, during the Silurian Age and reduce the planet to its component atoms. So T was born.

'We will have them,' one of the greatest Koax announced in triumph when the matter was thrashed out. 'Unless these ancient Earth records lie, and there is no reason why they should do, Sol originally supported nine planets, before its degenerate stage set in. Working inwards, in the logical order, these were – I have the names here, thanks to Man's sentimentality – Pluto, Neptune, Uranus, Saturn, Jupiter, Mars, Earth, Venus and Mercury. Earth, you see, is the seventh planet in, or the third that was drawn into Sol in its decline. That is our target, gentlemen, a speck remote in time and space. See that your calculations are accurate – that seventh planet *must* be destroyed.'

There was no error. The seventh planet was destroyed. Man never had any chance of detecting and blasting T and his eleven dark companions, for he had never discovered the mingled continuum in which they travelled. Their faint possibility of interception varied inversely with the distance they covered, for as they neared Man's first galaxy, time was rolled back to when he had first spiralled tentatively up to the Milky Way. The machines bore in and back. It was growing early. The Koax by now was a young race without the secret of deep space travel, dwindling away across the other side of the universe. Man himself had only a few old-type fluid fuel ships patrolling half a hundred systems. T still lay in his fixed position, waiting, waiting. His two centuries of existence – the long wait – were almost ended. Somewhere in his cold brain was a knowledge that the climax lay close now. Not all of his few companions were as fortunate, for the machines, perfect when they set out, developed flaws over the long journey (the two hundred years represented a distance in space/time of some ninety-five hundred million light years). The Koax were natural mathematical philosophers, but they had long ago given up being mechanics – otherwise they would have devised relay systems to manage the job that T had to do.

The nutrition feed in one machine slowly developed an increasing rate of supply, and the being died not so much from overeating as from growing pains – which were very painful indeed as he swelled again a bulkhead and finally sealed off the air vents with his own bulging flesh. In another machine, a transistor died, shorting the temporal drive; it broke through into real space and buried itself in an M-type variable sun. In a third, the guide system came adrift and the missile hurtled on at an increasing acceleration until it burnt itself out and fried its occupant. In a fourth, the occupant went quietly and unpredictably mad, and pulled a little lever that was not then due to be pulled for another hundred years. His machine erupted into fiery, radioactive particles and destroyed two other machines as well.

When the Solar System was only a few light years away, the remaining machines switched off their main drive and appeared in normal space/time. Only three of them had completed the journey, T and two others. They found themselves in a galaxy now devoid of life. Only the great stars shone on their new planets, fresh, comparatively speaking, from the womb of creation. Man had long before sunk back into the primaeval mud, and the suns and planets were nameless again. Over Earth, the mists of the early Silurian Age hovered, and in the shallows of its waters molluscs and trilobites were the only expression of life. Meanwhile T concentrated on the seventh planet. He had performed the few simple movements necessary to switch his machine back into the normal universe; now all that was left for him to do was to watch a small pressure dial. When the machine entered the atmospheric fringes of the seventh planet, the tiny hand on the pressure dial would begin to climb. When it reached a clearly indicated line on the dial, T would turn a small wheel (this would release the dampers – but T needed to know the How, not the Why). Then two more gauges would begin to register. When they both read the same, T had to

25

pull down the little lever. The speaker had explained all that to him regularly. What it did not explain was what happened after the lever was down, but T knew very well that then Man would be destroyed, and that that would be good.

The seventh planet swung into position ahead of the blunt bows of T's machine, and grew in apparent magnitude. It was a young world, with a future that was about to be wiped for ever off the slate of probability. As T entered its atmosphere, the hand began to climb the pressure dial. For the first time in his existence, something like excitement stirred in the fluid of T's brain. He neither saw nor cared for the panorama spreading below him, for the machine had not been constructed with ports. The dim instrument dials were all his eyes had ever rested on. He behaved exactly as the Koax had intended. When the hand reached top, he turned the damper wheel, and his other two gauges started to creep. By now he was plunging down through the stratosphere of the seventh planet. The load was planned to explode before impact, for as the Koax had no details about the planet's composition they had made certain that it went off before the machine struck and T was killed. The safety factor had been well devised. T pulled his last little lever twenty miles up. In the holocaust that immediately followed, he went out in a sullen joy.

T was highiy successful. The seventh planet was utterly obliterated. The other two machines did less brilliantly. One missed the Solar System entirely and went on into the depths of space, a speck with a patiently dying burden. The other was much nearer target. It swung in close to T and hit the sixth planet. Unfortunately, it detonated too high, and that planet, instead of being obliterated, was pounded into chunks of rock that took up erratic orbits between the orbits of the massive fifth planet and the eighth, which was a small body encircled by two tiny moons. The ninth planet, of course, was quite unharmed; it rolled serenely on, accompanied by its pale satellite and carrying its load of elementary life forms.

The Koax achieved what they had set out to do. They had calculated for the seventh planet and hit it, annihilating it utterly. But that success, of course, was already recorded on the only chart they had to go by. If they had read it aright, they would have seen . . . So, while the sixth was accidentally shattered, the seventh disappeared – Pluto, Neptune, Uranus, Saturn, Jupiter, the Asteroid planet, T's planet, Mars, Earth, Venus, Mercury – the seventh disappeared without trace.

On the ninth planet, the molluscs moved gently in the bright, filtering sunlight.

Our Kind of Knowledge

It was a glorious day for exploring the Arctic Circle. The brief and violent spring had exploded over the bleak lands with a welter of life. The wilderness was a wilderness of flowers. Flocks of tern and golden plover, with the world to sport in, stood here leg deep in blossom. Acres of blue ice crocus stretched away into the distance like shallow pools reflecting the clear skies. And on the near horizon rose a barrier of snow-covered mountains, high and harmless.

Five of them constituted the exploring party, the Preacher, Aprit, Woebee, Calurmo and Little Light, the Preacher being ahead as usual. They moved to the top of a rise, and there was the valley stretched before them, washed and brilliant. There too, was the spaceship.

Calurmo cried out in excitement and darted down among the flowers. The others saw instantly what was in his mind and followed fast behind, calling and laughing.

To them it was the most obvious feature of the colourful plain. Calurmo touched it first, and then they crowded around looking at it. The Preacher bent down and sniffed it.

'Yes,' he said. 'Definitely wood sorrel: *Oxalis acetosella*. How clever of it to grow up here.' His thoughts held a pious tinge; they always did: it was for that he bore the name Preacher.

Only afterwards did they notice the spaceship. It was very tall and sturdy and took up a lot of ground that might more profitably have been used by the flowers. It was also very heavy, and during the time it had stood there its stern had sunk into the thawing earth.

'A nice design,' Woebee commented, circling it. 'What do you think it is?'

High above their heads it towered. On the highest point sat a loon, preening itself in the sun and uttering occasionally its cry, the cry of emptiness articulate. Round the shadowed side of the ship, a shrivelled heap of snow rested comfortably against the metal. The metal was wonderfully smooth, but dark and unshining.

'However bulky it is down here, it manages to turn into a spire at the top,' the Preacher said, squinting, into the sun.

'But what is it?' Woebee repeated; then he began to sing, to show that he did not mind being unaware of what it was.

'It was *made*,' Aprit said cautiously. This was not like dealing with wood sorrel; they had never thought about spaceships before.

'You can get into it here,' Little Light said, pointing. He rarely spoke, and when he did he generally pointed as well.

They climbed into the airlock, all except Calurmo, who still stooped over the wood sorrel. Its fragrant pseudo-consciousness trembled with happiness in the fresh warmth of the sun. Calurmo made a slight churring noise, persistent and encouraging, and after a minute the tiny plant broke loose of the soil and crawled on to his hand.

He brought it up to his great eyes and let his thoughts slide gently in through the roots. Slowly they radiated up a stalk and into one of the yellow green trefoils, probing, exploring the sappy being of the leaf. Calurmo brought pressure to bear. Reluctantly, then with excitement, the plant yielded, and among its pink-streaked blossoms formed another, with five sepals, five petals, ten stamens and five stigmas, identical with the ones the plant had grown itself.

The tate of oxalic acid still pleasant in his thoughts, Calurmo sat back and smiled. To create a freak – that was nothing; but to create something just like the originals – how the others would be pleased!

'Calurmo!' It was Aprit, conspiratorial, almost guilty. 'Come and see what we've found.'

Knowing it would not be as delightful as the sorrel, nevertheless Calurmo jumped up, eager to share an interest. He climbed into the air lock and followed Aprit through the ship, carrying his flower carefully.

The others were drifting interestedly round the control room, high in the nose.

'Come and look at the valley!' invited Little Light, pointing out at the spread of bright land which shone all round them. From here, too, they could see a wide river, briefly shorn of ice and sparkling full of spawning fish.

'It's beautiful,' Calurmo said simply.

'We have indeed discovered a strange object,' remarked the Preacher, stroking a great upholstered seat. 'How old do you think it all is? It has the feel of great age.'

'I can tell you how long it has stood here,' said Woebee. 'The door through which we entered was open for the snow to drift in. When the snow melts it can never run away. I scanned it, and the earliest drops of it fell from the sky twelve thousand seasons ago.'

'What? Three thousand years?' exclaimed Aprit.

'No. Four thousand years – you know I don't count winter as a season.'

A line of geese broke V-formation to avoid the nose of the ship, and joined faultlessly again on the other side. Aprit caught their military thoughts as they sailed by.

'We should have come up this way more often,' said Calurmo regretfully, gazing at his sorrel. The tiny flowers were so very beautiful.

The next thing to decide was what they had discovered. Accordingly, they walked slowly round the control room, registering in unison, blithely unaware of the upper-level reasoning that lay behind their almost instinctive act. It took them five minutes, five minutes after starting completely from scratch: for the ship represented a fragment of a technology absolutely unknown to them. Also, it was a deep-spacer, which meant a corresponding complexity in drive, accommodation and equipment; but the particular pattern of its controls – repeated only in a few ships of its own class – designated unfailingly the functions and intentions of its vessel. At least, it did to Calurmo and party, and as easily as one may distinguish certain features of a hand from finding a lost glove.

Little surprise was wasted on the concept of a spaceship. As Aprit remarked, they had their own less cumbrous methods of covering interplanetary distances. But several other inferences fascinated them.

'Light is the fastest thing in our universe and the slowest in the dimension through which this ship travels,' said Woebee. 'It was made by a clever race.'

'It was made by a race incapable of carrying power in their own bodies,' said Little Light.

'Nor could they orient very efficiently,' the Preacher added, indicating the astro-navigational equipment.

'So there are planets attending other stars,' said Calurmo thoughtfully, his mind probing the possibilities.

'And sensible creatures on those planets,' said Aprit.

'Not sensible creatures,' said Little Light, pointing to the gunnery cockpit with its banks of switches. 'Those are to control destruction.'

'All creatures have some sense,' said the Preacher.

They switched on. The old ship seemed to creak and shudder, as if it had experienced too much time and snow ever to move again.

'It was content enough without stars,' muttered Woebee.

'Rainwater must have got into the hydrogen,' Aprit said.

'It's a very funny machine indeed to have made,' said the Preacher sternly. 'I don't wonder someone went away and left it.'

The boredom of manual control was not for them; they triggered the necessary impulses directly to the motors. Below them, the splendid plain tilted and shrank to a green penny set between the white and blue of land and sea. The edge of the ocean curved and with a breath-catching distortion became merely a segment of a great ball dwindling far beneath. The farther they got, the brighter it shone.

'Most noble view,' commented the Preacher.

Aprit was not looking. He had climbed into the computer and was feeding one of his senses along the relays and circuits of the memory bank and inference sector. He clucked happily as data drained to him. When he had it all he spat it back and returned to the others.

'Very ingenious,' he said, explaining it. 'But built by a race of behaviourists. Their souls were obviously trapped by their actions, consequently their science was trapped by their beliefs; they did not know where to look for real progress.'

'It's very noisy, isn't it?' remarked the Preacher, as if producing a point that confirmed what had just been said.

'That noise should not be,' said Calurmo coolly. 'It is an alarm bell, and indicates something is wrong.'

The sound played about them unceasingly until Aprit cut it off.

'I expect we are doing something wrong,' he sighed. 'I'll go and see what it is. But why make the bell ring here, and not where the trouble is?'

As Aprit left the control room, Little Light pointed into the huge celestial globe in which the stars of the galaxy were embalmed like diamonds in amber. 'Let's go there,' he suggested, rattling the calibrations until a tangential course lit up between Earth and a cluster of worlds in the centre of the galaxy. 'I'm sure it will be lovely there. I wonder if sorrel will grow in those parts; it won't grow on Venus, you know.'

While he spoke he spun the course integrator dial, read off the specifications of flight, and fed the co-ordinates as efficiently into the computer as if he had just undergone the (customary) two-year training course.

Aprit returned smiling.

'I've fixed it,' he said. 'Silly of us. We left the door open when we came in – there wasn't any air in here. That was why the bell was ringing.'

They were picked up on Second Empire screens about two parsecs from the outpost system of Kyla. An alert-beetle pinpointed them and flashed their description simultaneously to Main Base on Kyala I and half a dozen other interested points – a term including the needle fleet hovering two light years out from Kyla system.

Main Base to GOC Pointer, Needle Fleet 305A: Unidentified craft, mass 40,000 tons, proceeding outskirts system towards galaxy centre. Estimated speed, 20 SLU. Will you intercept?

GOC Pointer to Main Base, Kyla I: Am already on job.

Main Base to GOC Pointer: Alien acknowledges no signals, despite being called on all systems.

Pointer to Main Base: Quiet type. Appears to be heading from region Omega Y76 W592. Is this correct?

Main Base to Pointer: Correct.

Pointer to Main Base: Earth?

Main Base to Pointer: Looks like it.

Pointer to Main Base: Standing by for trouble.

Main Base to Pointer: Could be enemy stratagem, of course.

Pointer to Main Base: Of course. Going in. Out.

*　　*　　*

Officer Commanding needleship 'Pointer' was Grand-Admiral Rhys-Barley. He was still a youngish man, the Everlasting War being very good for promotion, but nevertheless thirty-four years of vacuum-busting lay behind him, sapping at his humanity. He stood now, purple of face under 4Gs, peering into the forward screens and snapping at Deeping.

Confusedly, Deeping flicked through the hand-view, trying to ignore the uniform that towered over him. On the handview, ship after ship appeared, only to be rejected by the selector. Here was trouble: the approaching alien, slipping in from a quarantined sector of space, could not be identified. The auto-view did not recognize it, and now old records were being checked on the handview; they, too, seemed to be drawing a blank.

Sweating, the unhappy Deeping glanced again at the image of the alien. Definitely not human; equally definitely, not Boux – or was it an enemy ruse, as Base suggested? The 'Pointer' was only half a parsec away from it now. They were within hitting distance, and the unidentified craft might hit first.

Fear, thought Deeping. My stomach is sick of the taste of fear: it knows all its nuances, from the numb terror of man's ancient enemy, the Boux, to the abject dread of Rhys-Barley's tongue. He flicked desperately. Suddenly the handview beeped.

The Grand-Admiral pounced, struck down the specificator bar and pulled out the emergent sheet. Even as he read it, a prolonged scrunching sound from the bowels of the ship announced that traction beams from 'Pointer' and a sister ship had interlocked on the speeding alien. The gravitics wavered for a moment under the extra load and then came back to normal.

'By Vega!' Rhys-Barley exclaimed, flourishing the flimsy under Captain Hardick's nose. 'What do you make of it? Tell Intake to go easy with our prize out there; they've got a bit of history on their hands. It's a First Empire ship, built something like four thousand seven hundred years ago on Luna, the satellite of Earth. Windsor Class, with a Spannell XII Light Drive. Ever hear of a Spannell Drive, Captain?'

'Before my day I'm afraid, sir.'

33

'Deeping, get Communications to have Kyla I send us details of all ships of Windsor Class, dates of obsolescence, etc. I think there's something queer ... Where'd it come from, I'd like to know.'

Interest made Rhys-Barley hop in front of the screens with less dignity than the Grand-Admiral usually mustered. Deeping relaxed enough to wink covertly at a friend on Bombardment Panel.

The alien was already visible through the ports as a gleaming chip a mile away, its terrific velocity killed by the traction beams. Now the tiny alert-beetle which had first discovered it made towards the 'Pointer'. The beetle gleamed pale red, scarcely visible against the regal profusion of Central stars. A beetle from the 'Pointer' shot out to meet it, bearing a cable. The beetles connected and floated back across the narrowing void. They touched the Windsor Class ship and instantly it was surrounded by the pale amber glow of a force shield.

Everyone on the 'Pointer' breathed more easily then. No energy whatsoever could break through that shield.

'Haul her in,' the Captain said.

Intake acknowledged the order and gradually the little ship was drawn closer.

Rhys-Barley cast an eye again at the encephalaphone reading on the bulkhead panel. Reading still 'Nil'. But the Nil wavered as if it was unsure of itself. Maybe they had caught a dead ship; thought waves should have registered before now, whether Boux or human.

Tension heightened again as the alien was drawn aboard. Matching velocities was a tricky business, and the manoeuvre always entailed a deal of noise audible throughout the ship. Pity super-science had never come up with a competent sound-absorber, Rhys-Barley thought morosely. The deck under him swayed a little.

Deeping handed him a slip from Kyla records. There had been four ships of the Windsor class. Three had gone to the scrap yards over three thousand years ago. The fourth had been abandoned for lack of fuel during the great Boux invasion waves that had resulted in the collapse of the First Empire. Its name: 'Regalia'.

'That must be our pigeon. Let's get down to Interrogation Bay, Captain,' Rhys-Barley suggested. Together the pair adjusted their arm-synchs and stepped into the teleport.

They reappeared instantly beside their captive. Aliens Officer was already there, enjoying a brief spell of glory, supervising the batteries of every type of recorder, scanner, probe and what-have-you the ship possessed in concealed positions about the 'Regalia'. The latter looked like a small whale stranded in a large cave.

The Preacher came first out of the air lock because he always went ahead anywhere. Then followed Calurmo and Aprit, stopping to examine the crystalline formations clinging to the lock doors. After them came Woebee and Little Light. Together they gazed at the severe functionalism and grey metal that surrounded them.

'This is not a pretty planet,' the Preacher observed.

'It is not the one Little Light chose,' Woebee explained.

'Don't be silly, the pair of you,' Calurmo said, a little sternly. 'This is not a planet. It is *made*. Use your senses.'

'Let's speak to those beings over there,' said Little Light, pointing. 'The one behind the invisibility screen.'

He wandered over to Rhys-Barley and tapped his rediffusion shield.

'I can see you,' he said. 'Can you see me?'

'All right, cut rediffusion,' snarled Rhys-Barley. The crimson on his face was no longer produced by the forces of gravity.

'No evidence of any energy or explosive weapons, sir,' Aliens Officer reported. 'Permission to interview?'

'OK.'

Aliens Officer wore a black uniform. His hair was white, his face was grey. He had a square jaw. The Preacher liked the look of him and approached.

'Are you the captain of this ship?' asked the Aliens Officer.

'That question does not mean anything to me, I'm sorry,' said the Preacher.

'Who commands this ship, the "Regalia"?'

'I don't understand that one either. What do you think he means, Calurmo?'

35

Calurmo was scanning the immense room in which they stood. His attention flicked momentarily to the little brain glands in the ceiling that computed the lung power present and co-ordinated the air supply accordingly. Then he explored all the minute currents and pulses that plied ceaselessly in the walls and floor, adjusting temperature and gravity, guarding against strain and metal fatigue; he swept the air itself, chemically pure and microbe-proof, rendered non-conductive. Nowhere did he find life, and for a moment he recalled the lands they had left, with the fish spawning in its rivers and the walrus sporting in its seas.

He dismissed the vision and tried to answer the Preacher's question.

'If he means who made the ship go, we all did,' he said. 'Little Light did the direction, Woebee and I did the fuel—'

'I don't like it in here, Calurmo,' Aprit interrupted. 'These beings smell of something odd . . .'

'It's fear,' said Calurmo, happy to be interrupted by a friend. 'Intellectual and physical fear. I'll tell you about it later. They've got some sort of inertia barrier up and their emotions don't come through, but their thoughts are clear enough.'

'Too clear!' said Woebee with a laugh. 'They are afraid of anyone who does not look like themselves, and if anyone *does* look like them – they are suspicious! I say, let's get back to the snows: that was a more interesting place to explore.'

He made a move towards the ship. Instantly an arrangement of duralum bars and R-rays descended from the roof and held them in five separate cells. They stood temporarily disconcerted in glowing cages.

The Aliens Officer walked among them grimly. 'Now you're going to answer questions,' he said. 'I'm sorry we are forced to use these methods to secure your attention. The speech-pattern separators that allow us to talk together work through the floor here and are relayed out to me via Main Base. I don't imagine you can do us much harm over such a system. And nothing can get through the electronic barricade we've brought up against you. In other words, you're trapped. Now let's have straight answers, please.'

· 'Here's a straight answer for your speech-pattern separator,' said April. Just for a second he wore a look of concentration. At once smoke rose from the floor of the bay. A dozen different alerts clicked and whirred, relentlessly bearing witness to ruined equipment.

Base signalled a two-day repair job required on language circuits.

'Now we'll use our system of communicating,' Aprit said, mollified.

'You shouldn't be destructive,' the Preacher reproved. 'Havoc becomes a habit.' Delighted with the chime of his maxim, he repeated it to himself.

Aliens Officer went a little paler. He recognized a show of force when he saw one. Also, he was still hearing them perfectly despite the smouldering failure of his speech-pattern separators. A subordinate hurried up and conferred with him for a moment. Then the officer looked up and said to the prisoners: 'At that act of destruction you released typical Boux configurations of thought. Do you admit your origins?'

Pointing to the R-rays, Little Light said: 'I am beginning to become uneasy, friends. This gadget surrounding us is as impervious as he claims.'

'I think it would be very wise to withdraw,' the Preacher agreed. 'Shall we not have left the Arctic?'

'That seems the only way,' agreed Calurmo doubtfully. Redature always upset his stomach.

Grand-Admiral Rhys-Barley pushed roughly forward. He was dissatisfied with the conduct of the interrogation. Also, he was worried. There was standard procedure for dealing with Boux; man's deadly enemy, originating on fast-rotating planets with high-velocity winds, were fluid in form and could easily assume the shape of men. A Boux-man loose on a planet like Kyla I could do an infinite amount of damage – and Boux-men were not easy to detect. Therefore, once Main Base was satisfied there were Boux aboard 'Pointer', they were quite likely to signal the flagship to proceed into the nearest sun. Rhys-Barley had other ideas about his future.

He halted pugnaciously before April.

'What's your real shape?' he demanded.

Aprit was puzzled. 'You mean my metaphysical shape?' he asked.

'No, I do not. I mean that my instruments register close to the Boux end of the brain impulse-scale. And Boux can masquerade as anything they like, over limited periods of time. What I'm asking is, who or what are you?'

'We are brothers,' said Aprit mildly. 'As you are our brother. Only you are a very bad-tempered brother.'

The stun was shot into Aprit's enclosure from the still-smoking floor. It struck with frightening suddenness. Pressure built instantaneously to a peak that would have spread a man uniformly over the walls of the enclosure in a pink paste. It would have forced a genuine Boux into one of his primary shapes. Aprit merely dropped unconscious to the deck.

Little Light pointed at the Grand-Admiral. 'For that, directly Aprit returns we shall not have left Arctic at all,' he said.

'It was a stupid and ignorant act,' agreed the Preacher.

Nobody had noticed Deeping. When the Captain and the Admiral had come through the teleport, he had been left to take the long, physical route down to Interrogation Bay. One does not waste six million volts on junior ranks.

Now he walked straight up to Calurmo and said, peering anxiously through the vibrating wall that separated them: 'I am very sorry we have not made you more welcome here, but we are at war.'

'Please don't apologize,' said Calurmo. 'It must be very upsetting for you to have a difference with someone. How long has this been happening?'

'Thousands of years,' said Deeping bitterly.

'March that man to the disintegrators,' Rhys-Barley bellowed. Two guards moved smartly towards Deeping.

'If you will pardon my venturing to suggest it,' Aliens Officer said, wobbling at the knees as he spoke, 'but just possibly, sir, this new approach might . . . might be effective.'

Faint with his own temerity, he saw Rhys-Barley's hand flicker and stay the guards.

'—a difference we can never settle until we vanquish the enemy,' Deeping was saying. He was still pale, but stood stiff

38

and resolute, almost as if he drew strength from these strange beings.

'Oh yes, you can settle it,' Calurmo said. 'But you've been going the wrong way about it.'

'Don't talk nonsense,' Rhys-Barley chimed in. 'You don't know the problem – unless you are a race of Boux we have not met before.'

'My friends are learning of the problem now,' murmured Calurmo, glancing at Little Light and Woebee, who were unusually quiet. But the Grand-Admiral went ruthlessly on.

'The enemy have inestimable advantages over Man. It has only been by exerting his military might up to the hilt, by standing continually on his toes, by having one finger perpetually on the trigger, that Man has kept the Boux out of his systems.'

'That really is the truth,' said Deeping earnestly. 'If you have a super-weapon you could let us know about we would be very grateful.'

'Don't humour me, please,' Calurmo said. He turned to Little Light and Woebee, who smiled and nodded. At the same time Aprit opened his eyes and stood up.

'I had such a funny dream,' he said. 'Do we go home now?'

'We want to readjust these people first,' the Preacher said. The five of them conferred together for a minute, while Rhys-Barley walked rapidly up and down and Deeping sneezed once or twice; R-rays had that effect on his nose.

Finally Woebee motioned to Deeping and said: 'You must forgive me if I say your people appear full of contradictions to us, but it is so. One contradiction, however, we could not understand. You pen us in here with impenetrable R-rays, as you term your inertia field, and also with duralum bars. The bars are quite superfluous unless – they are not what they seem. And of course they are not what they seem; they are another of the machines you so delight in. They are, in fact, categorizing grids that transmit almost comprehensive records of the five of us back to your nearest planet. An excellent device! Entire blueprints of us, psychologically and physiobiologically, are fed back to your biggest brain units. You really need complimenting on the efficiency of this machine. It is so good, in fact, that Little

Light and I have explored Main Base by it, have sent the rest of your fleet packing, and have broadcast directions to your vice-captain or whatever you call him up in the controls; as a result of which, you are now travelling where we want you to go and this Interrogation Bay is cut off from the rest of the ship.'

He had not finished speaking before Rhys-Barley had flung himself behind a shield and given the Emergency Destruction order. Nothing happened. Buttons, switches, valves, all were dead.

'You merely waste your time,' Little Light said, pointing at the Grand-Admiral and stepping through the dying R-rays. 'The power has gone. Did I not explain that clearly enough?'

'Where are you taking us?' Deeping whispered.

'You are taking *us*,' Woebee corrected.

'Not – not to Earth?'

Woebee smiled. 'I feel that the word "Earth" has some emotional value for you.'

'Gosh, yes, of course. Don't you see, it's the only planet we ever lost to the Boux, right at the beginning of our troubles with them. But Man came from there, Earth is Man's birth planet, and when it fell – that was the end of the First Empire. Since then we've grown stronger – but all that old peripheral region of space is dead ground to us now.'

Woebee nodded carelessly. 'We learned that from our investigation of Main Base. The area is now abandoned by the Boux too.'

'How awful to think of it stagnating all this time!' Deeping said.

'Really, you are as foolish as the rest,' said the Preacher reprovingly. 'The stagnation has been *here*. Why, you're still clinging to machinery to support you.'

He led his four friends back towards the 'Regalia'. 'We'll do the rest of the journey on our own,' he told them. 'These soldiers will want to go back to their duties. It's really none of our concern to hinder them!'

In the lock they paused. The personnel trapped in the Interrogation Bay looked bemused and helpless. Rhys-Barley sat on a step staring at the wall. The Captain bit his nails in an absorbed fashion.

Aliens Officer came forward and said: 'You have so much you could have taught us.'

'There's one piece of knowledge, unlike most of our kind of knowledge, that might be useful to you,' Aprit said casually. 'In Man's hurry to leave Earth because one or two Boux had arrived, some few men and women were left behind. They had no defence against the Boux, so the Boux had no need to attack them. In other words, there was an opportunity for – intermarriage.'

'Intermarriage!' echoed Aliens Officer.

'Yes,' the Preacher said solemnly. 'Neither you nor your machines seemed able to diagnose that. So you see our origins are a mixture of Man's and Boux's . . .'

'That is a priceless piece of knowledge,' Deeping reflected.

Calurmo smiled a valedictory smile that included even the deflated Admiral.

'I'm delighted if it proves so,' he said, 'but it is only a just return for Man's priceless gift to the Boux who were our distant ancestors: the gift of rigid form. Fluidity has proved a curse to the Boux. Intermarriage has recommendations for both sides. May I suggest you arrange – a love-match?'

This time he remembered to close the airlock doors. The 'Regalia' slid, apparently of its own volition, into the great lock of the 'Pointer' and out into space. By the time it was heading home, the flagship's captain was busy roaring at his bridge officers and Grand-Admiral Rhys-Barley was speaking apologetically to Base.

Deeping was staring at something that had materialized in his hand: wood sorrel, *Oxalis acetosella*. A flower from Earth.

Psyclops

Mmmm. I.

First statement: I am I. I am everything. Everything, everywhere. Every, every, every mmmm.

The universe is constructed of me, I am the whole of it. Am I? What is that regular throbbing that is not of me? That must be me too; after a while I shall understand it. All now is dim. Dim mmmm.

Even I am dim. In all this great strangeness and darkness of me, in all this universe of me. I am shadow. A memory of me. Could I be a memory of . . . not – me? Paradox: if I am everything, could there be a not-me, a somebody else?

Why am I having thoughts? Why am I not, as I was before, just mmmm?

Wake up! Wake up! It's urgent!

No! Deny it! I am the universe. If you can speak to me you must be me, so I command you to be still. There must be only the soothing, sucking mmmm.

. . . you are not the universe! Listen to me!

Louder?

For Heaven's sake, can you hear at last?

Non-comprehension. I must be everything. Can there be a part of me, like the throbbing, which is . . . separate?

Am I getting through? Answer!

Who . . . who are you?

Thank goodness you're receiving at last. Do not be frightened.

Are you another universe?

I am not a universe. You are not a universe. You are in danger and I must help you.

I am . . . Danger. No, curl, suck, mmmm! Only me in all the world. Disbelieve anything not me.

. . . must handle this carefully. Hell, what a task! Hey, stay awake there.

Mmmm. Must be mmmm . . .

. . . If only there was a psychofoetalist within light years of

here . . . Well, keep trying. Hey, wake up! You must wake up to survive!

Who are you?

I am your father.

Non-comprehension. Where are you? Are you the throbbing which is not me?

No. I am a long way from you. Light years away – oh hell! How do you start explaining?

Stop sending to me. You bring me feelings of . . . pain.

Catch hold of that idea of pain, son. Don't be afraid of it, but know there is much pain all about you. I am in constant pain.

Interest.

Good! First things first. You are most important.

I know that. All this is not happening. Somehow I catch these echoes, these dreams. I am *creating*; really, there is only me, entirely alone.

Try to concentrate. You are only one of millions like you. You and I are of the same species: human beings. I am born, you are unborn.

Meaningless.

Listen! Your 'universe' is inside another human being. Soon you will emerge into the real universe.

Still meaningless. Curious.

Keep alert. I will send you pictures to help you understand . . .

Uh . . .? Distance? Sight? Colour? Form? Definitely do not like this. Frightened. Frightened of falling, insecure . . . Must immediately retreat to safe mmmm. Mmmm.

Poor little blighter. Better let him rest! I'm half afraid of killing him. After all, he's only six months; at the Pre-natal Academies they don't begin rousing and education till seven and a half months. And then they're trained to the job. If only I knew – mind my leg, you blue swine!

That picture . . .

Oh, you're still there. Well done! I'm really sorry to rouse you so early, but it's vital.

Praise for me, warm feelings. Good. Nice. Better than being alone in the universe.

That's a great step forward, son. Huh, I can almost realize how the Creator felt, when you say that.

43

Non-comprehension.

Sorry, my fault: let the thought slip by. Must be careful. You were going to ask me about the picture I sent you. Shall I send again?

Only a little at once. Curious. Very curious. Shape, colour, beauty. Is that the real universe?

That was just Earth I showed you, where I was born, where I hope you will be born.

Non-comprehension. Show again ... shapes, tones, scents. ... Ah, this time not so strange. Different?

Yes, a different picture. Many pictures of Earth, look.

Ah ... Better than my darkness ... I know only my darkness, sweet and warm, yet I seem to remember those – trees.

That's a race memory, son. We're doing well. Your faculties are beginning to work now.

More beautiful pictures please.

We cannot waste too long on the pictures. I've got a lot to tell you before you get out of range. And – hello, what are we stopping for now? These blue devils—

Why do you cease sending so abruptly? Hello? ... Nothing. Father? ... Nothing. Was there ever anything, or have I been alone and dreaming?

Nothing in all my universe but the throbbing. Throbbing near me. Is someone here with me? Hello? No, no answer. I must ask the voice, if the voice comes back. Now I must mmmm. Am no longer content as I was before. Strange feelings ... I want more pictures; I want ... to ... be ... alive. No, must mmmm.

Mmmm.

Dreaming myself to be a fish, fin-tailed, flickering through deep, still water. All is green and warm and without menace, and I swim for ever with assurance ... And then the water splits into lashing cords and plunges down, down, down a sunlit cliff. I fight to turn back, carried forward, fighting to return to the deep, sure dark—

—if you want to save yourself! Wake if you want to save yourself! I can't hold out much longer. Another few days across those damned mountains—

Go away! Leave me to myself. I can have nothing to do with you.

44

My dear babe! You must try and understand. I know it's agony for you, but you must stir yourself and take in what I say. It is imperative.

Nothing is imperative here. Yet he said 'race memories'. And now my mind seems to clear. Yes! I exist in the darkness of my head where formerly there was nothing. Yes, there are imperatives; that I can recognize. Father?

What are you trying to say?

Confused. Understanding better, trying harder, but so confused. And there is always the throbbing by my side.

Do not worry about that. It is your twin sister. The Pollux II hospital diagnosed twins, one boy and one girl.

Always so many concepts I cannot grasp. I should despair, but for curiosity prodding me on. Explain first 'boy' and 'girl' and 'twin sister'.

At a time like this! Well, we humans are divided into two sexes for purposes of continuing the race. These two sexes are called 'boys' and 'girls', and for convenience it has been decided that the small continuations – like you – should be carried inside the girls until they are strong enough to exist alone. Sometimes the little continuations are alone, sometimes they come in pairs, sometimes three or even more together.

And I'm one of a pair?

There you have it. That is a little girl lying next to you; you can hear her heart beating. Your mother—

Stop, stop! Too much to understand at once. Must think to myself about this. Will call you back.

Don't be long. Every minute takes you farther from me . . .

Must keep a hold on myself. My brain reels. Everything so strange! And my universe shrunken to a womb. Numb, just feel numb. Cannot manage to cope with any more. Numb. Mmmm.

Back into the deep dark, soothed and suckled. Now I am a fish, twinkling smoothly through the uncrumpled water. Everything here calm, but ahead – The brink! I turn tail and flip back – too late, too late.

Hey, don't panic there. It's only me!

Danger, you said danger.

*Keep calm and take it easy. There is something you must
do for me – for us all. If you do that, there is no danger.*

Tell me quickly.

*As yet it is too difficult. In a few days you will be ready –
if I can hang out that long.*

Why is it difficult?

Only because you are small.

Where are you?

*I am on a world rather like Earth which is ninety light
years from Earth and getting farther from you even as we
communicate together.*

Why? How? Don't understand. So much is now beyond
my understanding; before you came everything was peaceful
and dim.

*Lie quiet and don't fret, son. You're doing well: you take
the points quickly, you'll reach Earth yet. You are travelling
towards Earth in a spaceship which left Mirone, the planet
where I am, sixteen days ago.*

Send that picture of a spaceship again.

Coming up . . .

It is a kind of metal womb for us all. That idea I can more
or less grasp, but you don't explain distances to me satisfac-
torily.

*These are big distances, what we call light years. I can't
picture them for you properly because a human mind never
really grasps them.*

Then they don't exist.

*Unfortunately they exist all right. But they are only com-
prehensible as mathematical concepts. OHHH! My leg . . .*

Why are you stopping? I remember you suddenly stopped
before. You send a horrible pain thought, then you are gone.
Answer.

Wait a minute.

I can hardly hear you. Now I am interested, why do you
not continue? Are you there?

*. . . this is all beyond me. We're all finished. Judy, my love,
if only I could reach you . . .*

Who are you talking to? Answer me at once! This is all so
frustrating. You are so faint and your message so blurred.

Call you when I can . . .

Fear and pain. Only symbols from his mind to mine, yet

they have an uncomfortable meaning of their own – something elusive. Perhaps another race memory.

My own memory is not good. Un-used. I must train it. Something he said eludes me; I must try and remember it. Yet why should I bother? None of it really concerns me, I am safe here, safe for ever in this darkness.

That was it! There is another here with me, a sister. Why does he not send to her? Perhaps I could send to her; she is nearer to me than he is.

Sister! Sister! I am calling you. The throbbing comes from her but she does not answer.

This whole thing is imagination. I am talking to myself. Wait! Like a distant itch I can feel his projections coming back again. Do not trouble to listen to his riddles.

Curious.

... gangrene, without doubt. Shall be dead before these blue devils get me to their village. So much Judy and I planned to do ...

Are you listening, son?

No, no.

Listen carefully while I give you some instructions.

Have something to ask you.

Please save it. The connection between us is growing attenuated: soon we will be out of mind range.

Indifferent.

My dear child, how could you be other than indifferent! I am truly sorry to have broken so early into your foetal sleep.

An unnameable sensation, half-pleasant: gratitude, love? No doubt a race memory.

It may be so. Try to remember me – later. Now, business. Your mother and I were on our way back to Earth when we stopped on this world Mirone, where I now am. It was an unnecessary luxury to break our journey. How bitterly now I wish we had never stopped.

Why did you?

Well, it was chiefly to please Judy – your mother. This is a beautiful world, round the North Pole, anyhow. We had wandered some way from the ship when a group of natives burst out upon us.

Natives?

People who live here. They are sub-human, blue-skinned and hairless – not at all pretty to look at.

Picture!

I think you'd be better without one. Judy and I ran like mad for the ship. We were nearly up to it when a rock caught me behind the knee – they were pitching rocks at us – and I went down. Judy never noticed until she was in the air lock, and then the savages were on me. My leg was hurt; I couldn't even put up a fight.

Please tell me no more of this. It makes me ill. I want mmmm.

Listen, son, don't cut off! That's all the frightening part. I called to Judy to make off home, so she and you and your sister got safely away. The savages are taking me over the mountains to their village. I don't think they mean to harm me; I'm just a . . . curiosity to them.

Please let me mmmm.

You can go comatose as soon as I've explained how these little space craft work. Astrogating, the business of getting from one planet to another, is far too intricate a task for anyone but an expert to master. I'm not an expert, I'm a geohistorian. So the whole thing is done by a robot pilot. You feel it details like payload, and gravities and destination, and it juggles them with the data in its memory banks and works out all the course for you – carries you home safely, in fact. Do you get all that?

This sounds a very complicated procedure.

Now you're talking like your mother, boy. She's never bothered, but actually it's all simple stuff: the complications take place under the steel panelling where you don't worry about them. The point I'm trying to make is that steering is all automatic once you've punched in a few co-ordinates.

I'm dead tired.

So am I. Fortunately, before we left the ship that last time, I had set up the figures for Earth. OK?

If you had not, she would not have been able to get home?

Exactly it. You have your father's brains, kid. Keep trying! She left Mirone safely and you are now all heading for Earth – but you'll never make it. When I set the figures up, they were right; but my not being aboard made them wrong. Every split second of thrust the ship makes is calculated for an extra eleven and a half stone that isn't there. It's here with me, being hauled along a mountain.

Is this bad? Except, I mean, for you. Does it mean we reach Earth travelling too fast?

No, son. IT MEANS YOU'LL NEVER REACH EARTH AT ALL. The ship moves in a hyperbola, and although my weight is only about one eight thousandth of total ship's mass, that tiny fraction of error will have multiplied itself into a couple of light years by the time you get adjacent to the solar system.

I'm trying, but this talk of distance means nothing to me. Explain it again.

Where you are there is neither light nor space; how do I make you feel what a light year is? No, you'll just have to take it from me that the crucial point is, you'll shoot right past the Earth.

Can't we go on till we hit another planet?

You will – if nothing is done about it. But landfall will be delayed some odd thousands of years.

You are growing fainter. Strain too much. Must mmmm.

The fish again, and the water deep about him. No peace in the pool now. Cool pool, cruel pool, pool ... The waters whirl towards the brink.

I am the fish-foetus. Have I dreamed? Was there a voice talking to me? It seems unlikely. And if it spoke, did it speak truth? Something I had to ask it, one gigantic fact which made nonsense of everything; something – Ah, cannot remember. Could refute everything if I could remember that.

Perhaps there was no voice. Perhaps in this darkness I have taken a wrong turning in my development: a wrong choice between sanity and non-sanity. Then my first thoughts may have been correct. I am everything and I am mad!

Help! Speak to me, speak!

No reply. The throbbing only. *That* was the question—

... thank heavens for hot spring water ...

Hello! Father?

How long will they let me lie here in this pool? They must realize I'm not long for this world, or any other.

I'm awake and answering!

Just let me lie here. Son, it's man's first pleasure and his last to lie and swill in hot water. Wish I could live to know you ... However. To work. Here's what you have to do to get out of this present jam.

Am powerless here. Unable to do anything.

Don't get frightened. There's something you already do very expertly: telemit.

Non-comprehension.

We talk to each other over this growing distance by what is called telepathy. It's part gift, part skill. It happens to be the only contact between distant planets, except spaceships. But whereas spaceships take time to get anywhere, thought is instantaneous.

Understood.

Good. Unfortunately, whereas spaceships get anywhere in time, thought has a definite limited range. Its span is as strictly governed as – well, as the size of a plant, for instance. When you are fifty light years from Mirone, contact between us will abruptly cease.

What stops thought?

I don't know, any more than I could tell you what started it to begin with.

Other obvious questions: how far apart are we now?

At the most we have forty-eight hours more in contact.

Don't leave me. I shall be lonely!

I'll be lonely too – but not for long. But you, son, you are already half-way to Earth, or as near as I can estimate it you are. As soon as contact between us ceases, you must call TRE.

Which means?

Telepath Radial Earth. It's a general control and information centre, permanently beamed for any sort of emergency. You can raise them. I can't.

They won't know me.

I'll give you their call pattern. They'll soon know you when you telemit. You can give them my pattern for identification if you like. You must explain what is happening.

Doubtful.

You can explain, can't you? – About your missing Earth altogether?

Will they believe?

Of course.

Are they real?

Of course.

Hard to believe in more people than just us. I had a question—

Just a minute, let's get this sorted out. Tell TRE what the trouble is; they'll send out a fast ship to pick Judy and you up before you are out of range.

Yes, now I have it. I want to ask you that question. Voice—

Wait a minute, son ... You're going too faint, or is that me? ... Can you smell the gangrene over all those light years? ... These blue horrors are lifting me out of the spring, and I'll probably pass out. Not much time ...

Father, what is this 'time' that seems to mean so much to you?

... time like an ever-rolling stream bears all her sons ... Aaah ... Time, son, never enough time ...

Pain. Pain and silence. Revulsion in me. Can the universe be as horrible and confusing as he would have me think? All like a dream.

Mmmm. Long silence and darkness. Voice gone. Strain. Try.

... distance ...

Voice! Father! Louder!

... too feeble ... Done all I could ...

Tell me just one thing, Father!

Quickly.

Was it difficult to rouse me at first?

Yes. In the Pre-natal Academies foetuses are not roused for training and indoctrination until they are seven and a half months old. But this was an emergency. I had to ... oh, I'm too weary—

Then why did you rouse me and not communicate with my mother?

The village! We're nearly there. Just down into the valley

51

and it's journey's end ... Human race only developing tele-
pathic powers, gradually ... Steady, you fellows!

The question, answer the question.

That is the answer. Easy down the slope, boys. Don't want
to burst this great big leg, eh? Er ... I had the ability but
Judy hadn't; I couldn't call her a yard away. But you've got
the ability. Easy, oh! All the matter in the universe is in my
leg ...

But why – you sound so muddled – why—?

Good old Mendelian theory ... You and your sister, one
sensitive, one not. Two eyes of the giant and only one can
see properly ... the path's too steep to – whoa, Cyclops,
steady, boy, or you'll put out that other eye.

Cannot understand!

, *Understand? My leg's a flaming torch – put out anyone's*
eye. Steady, steady! Gently down the steep blue hill.

Father!

What's the matter?

I can't understand. Are you talking of real things?

Sorry, boy. Steady now. Touch of delirium; it's the pain.
You'll be OK if you get in contact with TRE. Remember?

Yes, I remember. If only I could ... I don't know. Mother
is *real* then?

Yes. You must look after her.

And is the giant real?

The giant? What giant? You mean the giant hill. The
people are climbing up the giant hill. Up to my giant leg.
Good-bye, son. I've got to see a blue man about a ... a leg
... a leg ...

Father!

... a leg of blue mutton ...

Father, where are you going? Wait, wait, look, see, I can
move a little. I've just discovered I can *turn*. Father!

No answer now. Just a tiny stream of silence and the
throbbing. And the throbbing. My silent sister. She can't
think like I can. I have got to call TRE.

Plenty of time. Perhaps if I *turn* first ... Easy. I'm only six
months, he said. Maybe I could call more easily if I was
outside, in the real universe. If I turn again.

Now if I *kick* ...

Ah, easy now. Kick again. Good. Wonder, if my legs are blue.

Kick.

Good. Something yielding.

Kick ...

Conviction

The four Supreme Ultralords stood apart from the crowd, waiting, speaking to nobody. Yet Mordregon, son of Great Mordregon; Arntibis Isis of Sirius III, the Proctor Superior from the Tenth Sector; Deln Phi J. Bunswacki, Ruler of the Margins; and Ped² of the Dominion of the Sack watched, as did the countless other members of the Diet of the Ultralords of the Home Galaxy, the entrance into their council chamber of the alien, David Stevens of Earth.

Stevens hesitated on the threshold of the hall. The hesitation was part-natural, part-feigned; he had come here primed to play a part and knowing a pause for awe might be expected of him; but he had not calculated on the real awe which filled him. He had come to stand trial, for himself, for Earth, he had come prepared – as far as a man may prepare for the unpredictable. Yet, as the dolly ushered him into the hall, he knew crushingly that the task was to be more terrible than any he had visualized.

The cream of the Galaxy took in his hesitation.

He started to walk towards the dais upon which Mordregon and his colleagues waited. The effort of forcing his legs to go into action set a dew of perspiration on his forehead.

'God help me!' he whispered. But these were the gods of the galaxy; was there, over them, One with no material being and infinite power? Enough. Concentrate.

Squaring his shoulders, Stevens walked between the massed shapes of the rulers of the Home Galaxy. Although it had been expressly stated before he left Earth that no powers, such as telepathy, which he did not possess, would be used against him, he could feel a weight of mental power all round him. Strange faces watched him, some just remotely human, strange robes stirred as he brushed past them. The diversity! he thought. The astounding, teeming womb of the universe!

Pride suddenly gripped him. He found courage to stare

back into the multitudinous eyes. They should be made to know the mettle of man. Whatever they were planning to do with him, he also had his own plans for them.

Just as it seemed only fitting to him that man should walk in this hall, it seemed no less fitting that of all the millions on Earth, he, David Stevens, should be that man. With the ego-tism inherent in junior races, he felt sure he could pass their trial. What if he had been awed at first? A self-confident technological civilization, proud of its exploration projects on Mercury and Neptune, is naturally somewhat abashed by the appearance of a culture spreading luxuriously over fifty hundred thousand planets.

With a flourish, he bowed before Mordregon and the other Supreme Ultralords.

'I offer greetings from my planet Earth of Sol,' he said in a resonant voice.

'You are welcome here, David Stevens of Earth,' Mordregon replied graciously. A small object the size of a hen's egg floated fifteen inches from his beak. All other members of the council, Stevens included, were attended by similar devices, automatic interpreters.

Mordregon was mountainous. Below his beaked head, his body bulged like an upturned grand piano. A cascade of clicking black and white ivory rectangles clothed him. Each rectangle, Stevens noted, rotated perpetually on its longi-tudinal axis, fanning him, ventilating him, as if he burned continually of an inexorable disease (which was in fact the case).

'I am happy to come here in peace,' Stevens said. 'And shall be still happier to know why I have been brought here. My journey has been long and partially unexplained.'

At the word 'peace', Mordregon made a grimace like a smile, although his beak remained unsmiling.

'Partially, perhaps; but partially is not entirely,' Mordregon said. 'The robot ship told you you would be col-lected to stand trial in the name of Earth. That seems to us quite sufficient information to work on.'

The automatic translators gave an edge of irony to the Utralord's voice. The tone brought faint colour to Stevens's cheeks. He was angry, and suddenly happy to let them see he was angry.

'Then you have never been in my position,' he said. 'Mine was an executive post at Port Ganymede. I never had anything to do with politics. I was down at the methane reagent post when your robot ship arrived and designated me in purely arbitrary fashion. I was simply told I would be collected for trial in three months – like a convict – like a bundle of dirty laundry!'

He looked hard at them, anxious to see their first reaction to his anger, wondering whether he had gone too far. Ordinarily, Stevens was not a man who indulged his emotions. When he spoke, the hen's egg before his mouth sucked up all sound, leaving the air dry and silent, so that he was unable to hear the translation going over; he thought, half-hopefully, that it might omit the outburst in traditional interpreter fashion. This hope was at once crushed.

'Irritation means unbalance,' said Deln Phi J. Bunswacki. It was the only sentence he spoke throughout the interview. On his shoulders, a mighty brain siphoned its thoughts beneath a transparent skull case; he wore what appeared to be a garishly cheap blue pin-stripe suit, but the stripes moved as symbiotic organisms plied up and down them ceaselessly, ingurgitating any microbes which might threaten the health of Deln Phi J. Bunswacki.

Slightly revolted, Stevens turned back to Mordregon.

'You are playing with me,' he said quietly. 'Do I abuse your hospitality by asking you to get down to business?'

That, he thought, was better. Yet what were they thinking? *His manner is too unstable? He seems to be impervious to the idea of his own insignificance?* This was going to be the whole of hell: to have to guess what *they* were thinking, knowing they knew he was guessing, *not* knowing how many levels above his own their IQ was.

Acidic apprehension turned in Stevens's stomach. His hand fluttered up to the lump below his right ear; he fingered it nervously, and only with an effort broke off the betraying gesture. To this vast concourse, he *was* insignificant: yet to Earth – to Earth he was their sole hope. Their sole hope! – And he could not keep himself from shaking.

Mordregon was speaking again. What had he been saying?

'... customary. Into this hall in the city of Grapfth on the planet Xaquibadd in the Periphery of the Dominion of the Sack are invited all new races, each as it is discovered.'

Those big words don't frighten me, Stevens told himself, because, to a great extent, they did. Suddenly he saw the solar system as a tiny sack, into which he longed to crawl and hide.

'Is this place Grapfth the centre of your Empire?' he asked.

'No; as I said, it is in a peripheral region – for safety reasons, you understand,' Mordregon explained.

'Safety reasons? You mean you are afraid of me?'

Mordregon raised a brow at Ped^2 of the Sack. Ped^2, under an acre of coloured, stereoscopic nylon, was animated cactus, more beautiful, more intricate than his clothing. Butterflies captive on degravitized geranium chains turned among the blossoms on his head; they fluttered up and then re-alighted as Ped^2 nodded and spoke briefly to the Earthman. 'Every race has peculiar talents or abilities of its own,' he explained. 'It is partly to discover those abilities that you aliens are invited here. Unfortunately, your predecessor turned out to be a member of a race of self-propagating nuclear weapons left over from some ancient war or other. He talked quite intelligently, until one of us mentioned the key word "goodwill", whereupon he exploded and blew this entire hall to bits.'

Reminiscent chuckles sounded round him as he told the story.

Stevens said angrily: 'You expect me to believe that? Then how have you all survived?'

'Oh, we are not really here,' Ped^2 said genially, interlocking a nest of spikes behind his great head. 'You can't expect us to make the long journey to Xaquibadd every time some petty little system – no offence of course – is discovered. You're talking to three-dimensional images of us; even the hall's only there – or *here*, if you prefer it (location is merely a philosophical quibble) in a sort of sub-molecular fashion.'

Catching sight of the dazed look on the Earthman's face, Ped^2 could not resist driving home another point. (His was a childish race: theologians had died out among them only some four thousand years ago.)

'We are not even talking to you in a sense you would understand, David Stevens of Earth,' he said. 'Having as yet no instantaneous communicator across light-year distances, we are letting a robot brain on Xaquibadd do the talking for us. We can check with it afterwards; if a mistake has been made, we can always get in touch with you.'

It was said not without an easy menace, but Stevens received at least a part of it eagerly. They had as yet no instantaneous communicator! No sub-radio, that could leap light years without time lag! Involuntarily, he again fingered the tiny lump beneath the lobe of his right ear, and then thrust his hand deep into his pocket. So Earth had a chance of bargaining with these colossi after all! His confidence soared.

To Ped², Mordregon was saying: 'You must not mock our invited guest.'

'I have heard that word "invited" from you before,' Stevens said. 'This has all seemed to me personally more like a summons. Your robot, without further explanation, simply told me it would be back for me in three months, giving me time to prepare for trial.'

'That was reasonable, surely?' Mordregon said. 'It *could* have interviewed you then, unprepared.'

'But it didn't say what I was to prepare *for*,' Stevens replied, exasperation bursting into his mind as he remembered those three months. What madness they had been, as he spent them preparing frantically for this interview; all the wise and cunning men of the system had visited him: logicians, actors, philosophers, generals, mathematicians ... And the surgeons! Yes, the skilful surgeons, burying the creations of the technologists in his ear and throat.

And all the while he had marvelled: Why did they pick *me?*

'Supposing it *hadn't* been me?' he said to Mordregon aloud. 'Supposing it had been a madman or a man dying of cancer you picked on?'

Silence fell. Mordregon looked at him piercingly and then answered slowly: 'We find our random selection principle entirely satisfactory, considering the large numbers involved. Whoever is brought here is responsible for his world. Your mistakes or illnesses are your world's mistakes or illnesses. If a madman or a cancerous man stood in your place now, your world would have to be destroyed; worlds which have not been made free from such scourges by the time they have interplanetary travel must be eradicated. The galaxy is indestructible, but the security of the galaxy is a fragile thing.'

All the light-heartedness seemed gone from the assembly of Ultralords now. Even Ped[2] of the Dominion of the Sack sat bolt upright, looking grimly at the Earthman. Stevens himself had gone chill, his throat was as dry as his sleeve. Every time he spoke he betrayed a chunk of the psychological atmosphere of Earth.

During the three months' preparation, during the month-long voyage here in a completely automatic ship, he had chased his mind round to come only to this one conclusion: that through him Man was to be put to a test for fitness. Thinking of the mental homes and hospitals of Earth, his poise almost deserted him; but clenching his fists together behind his back – what matter if the assembly saw that betrayal of strain, so long as the searching eyes of Mordregon did not? – he said in a voice striving to remain firm: 'So then I *have* come here on trial?'

'Not you only but your world Earth – and the trial has already begun!' The voice was not Mordregon's nor Ped[2]'s. It belonged to Arntibis Isis of Sirius III, the Proctor Superior of the Tenth Sector, who had not yet spoken. He stood like a column, twelve feet high, his length clad in furled silver, a dark cluster of eyes at his summit probing down at Stevens. He had what the others, what even Mordregon lacked: majesty.

Surreptitiously, Stevens touched his throat. The device nestling there would be needed presently; with its assistance he might win through. This Empire had no sub-radio; in that fact lay his and Earth's hope. But before Arntibis Isis hope seemed stupidity.

'Since I am here I must necessarily submit to your trial,' Stevens said. 'Although where I come from, the civilized thing is to tell the defendant *what* he is defending, *how* he may acquit himself and *which* punishment is hanging over

59

his head. We also have the courtesy to announce when the trial begins, not springing it on the prisoner half-way through.'

A murmur circling round the hall told him he had scored a minor point. As Stevens construed the problem, the Ultralords were looking for some cardinal virtue in man which, if Stevens manifested it, would save Earth; but which virtue did this multicoloured mob consider important? He had to pull his racing mind up short to hear Arntibis Isis's reply to his thrust.

'You are talking of a local custom tucked away in a barren pocket of the galaxy,' the level voice said. 'However, your intellect being what it is, I shall enumerate the how and the wherefore. Be it known then, David Stevens of Earth, that through you your world is on trial before the Supreme Diet of the Ultralords of the Second Galaxy. Nothing personal is intended: indeed, you yourself are barely concerned in our business here, except as a mouthpiece. *If* you acquit yourself – and we are more than impartial, we are eager for your success, though less than hopeful – your race Man will become Full Fledgling Members of our great concourse of human beings, sharers of our skills and problems. If you fail, your planet Earth will be annihilated – utterly.'

'And you call that civilized—?' Stevens began hotly.

'We deal with fifty planets a week here,' Mordregon interrupted. 'It's the only possible system – cuts down endless bureaucracy.'

'Yes, and we just can't afford fleets to watch these unstable communities any more,' one of the Ultralords from the body of the hall concurred. 'The expense . . .'

'Do you remember that ghastly little time-swallowing reptile from somewhere in the Magellans?' Ped[2] chuckled reminiscently. 'He had some crazy scheme for a thousand years' supervision of his race.'

'I'd die of boredom if I watched them an hour,' Mordregon said; shuddering.

'Order, please!' Arntibis Isis snapped. When there was silence, he said to Stevens: 'And now I will give you the rules of the trial. Firstly, there is no appeal from our verdict; when the session is over, you will be transported back to

Earth at once, and the verdict will be delivered almost as soon as you land there.

'Next, I must assure you we are scrupulously fair in our decision, although you must understand that the definition of fairness differs from sector to sector. You may think we are ruthless; but the Galaxy is a small place and we have no room for useless members within our ranks. As it is we have this trouble with the Eleventh Galaxy on our hands. However ...

'Next, many of the beings present have powers which you would regard as supernormal, such as telepathy, deepvision, precognition, outfarling, and so on. These powers they are holding in abeyance, so that you are judged on your own level as far as possible. You have our assurance that your mind will not be read.

'There is but one other rule; you will now proceed with your trial.'

For a space of a few chilly seconds, Stevens stared unbelievingly at the tall column of Arntibis Isis: that entity told him nothing. He looked round at Mordregon, at the others, at the phalanx of figures silent in the hall. Nobody moved. Gazing round at the incredible sight of them, Stevens realized sadly how far, far from home he was.

'... my own trial?' he echoed.

The Ultralords did not reply. He had had all the help, if help it was; now he was on his own: Earth's fate was in the scales. Panic threatened him but he fought it down; that was a luxury he could not afford. Calculation only would help him. His cold hand touched the small lump at his throat; his judges had, after all, virtually played into his hands. He was not unprepared.

'My own trial,' he repeated more firmly.

Here was the classic nightmare made flesh, he thought. Dreams of pursuit, degradation, annihilation were not more terrible than this static dream where one stands before watchful eyes explaining one's existence, speaking, speaking to no avail because if there is right it is not in words, because if there is a way of delivering the soul it is not to this audience. He thought, I must all my life have had some sort of a

61

fixation about judgment without mercy; now I've gone psychopathic – I'll spend all my years up before this wall of eyes, trying to find excuses for some crime I don't know I've committed.

He watched the slow revolutions of Mordregon's domino costume. No, this was reality, not the end results of an obsession. To treat it as other than reality was the flight from fear; that was not Stevens's way: he was afraid, but he could face it.

He spoke to them.

'I presume by your silence,' he said, 'that you wish me to formulate both the questions and the answers, on the principle that two differing levels of intelligence are thus employed; it being as vital to ask the right question as to produce the correct answer.

'This forcing of two roles upon me obviously doubles my chance of failure, and I would point out that this is, to me, not justice but a mockery.

'Should I, then, say nothing more to you? Would you accept that silence as a proof that my world can distinguish justice from injustice, surely one of the prime requisites of a culture?'

He paused, only faintly hopeful. It could not be as simple as that. Or could it? If it could the solution would seem to him just a clever trick; but to these deeper brains it might appear otherwise. His thoughts swam as he tried to see the problem from their point of view. It was impossible: he could only go by his own standards, which of course was just what they wanted. Yet still he kept silence, trusting it more than words.

'Your point accepted. Continue,' said Ped²
brusquely, but he gave Stevens an encouraging nod.

So it was not going to be as easy as that. He pulled a handkerchief from a pocket and wiped his forehead, thinking wildly: 'Would they accept *that* as a defence: that I am near enough to the animal to sweat but already far enough away to object to the fact? Do they sweat, any of them? Perhaps they think sweat's a good thing. How can I be sure of anything?'

Like every other thought to his present state of mind, it turned circular and short-circuited itself.

He was an Earthman, six foot three, well proportioned, he had made good in a tough spot on Ganymede, he knew a very lovely woman called Edwina. Suppose they would be content with hearing about her, about her beauty, about the way she looked when Stevens left Earth. He could tell them about the joy of just being alive and thinking of Edwina: and the prodding knowledge that in ten years their youth would be sliding away.

Nonsense! he told himself. They wouldn't take sentiment here; these beauties wanted cold fact. Momentarily, he thought of all the other beings who had stood in the past where he stood now, groping for the right thing to say. How many had found it?

Steadying himself, Stevens began to address the Ultralords again.

'You will gather from what I say that I am hoping to demonstrate that I possess and understand one virtue so admirable that because of it you will, in your wisdom, be able to do nothing but spare me. Since modesty happens to be one of my virtues, I cannot enumerate the others: sagacity, patience, courage, loyalty, reverence, kindness, for example – and humour, as I hope that remark may hint to you. But these virtues are, or should be, common possessions of any civilization; by them we define civilization, and you presumably are looking for something else.

'You must require me to produce evidence of something less obvious ... something Man possesses which none of you have.'

He looked at the vast audience and they were silent. That damned silence!

'I'm sure we do possess something like that. I'll think of it if you'll give me time. (Pause.) I suppose it's no good throwing myself on your mercy? Man has mercy – but that's not a virtue at all acceptable to those without it.'

The silence grew round him like ice forming over a Siberian lake. Were they hostile or not? He could not tell anything from their attitude; he could not think objectively. Reverse that idea: he thought subjectively. Could he twist *that* into some sort of a weird virtue which might appeal to them, and pretend there was a special value in thinking subjectively?

Hell, this was not his line of reasoning at all; he was not cut out to be a metaphysician. It was time he played his trump card. With an almost imperceptible movement of a neck muscle, he switched on the little machine in his throat. Immediately its droning awoke, reassuring him.

'I must have a moment to think,' Stevens said to the assembly.

Without moving his lips, he whispered: *'Hello, Earth, are you there, Earth? Dave Stevens calling across the light-years. Do you hear me?'*

After a moment's pause, the tiny lump behind his ear throbbed and a shadowy voice answered: *'Hello, Stevens, Earth Centre here. We've been listening out for you. How are you doing?'*

'The trial is on. I don't think I'm making out very well.' His lips were moving slightly; he covered them with his hand, standing as if deep in cogitation. It looked, he thought, very suspicious. He went on: *'I can't say much. For one thing, I'm afraid they will detect this beam going out and regard our communication as infringing their judicial regulations.'*

'You don't have to bother about that, Stevens. You should know that a sub-radio beam is undetectable. Can we couple you up with the big brain as pre-arranged? Give it your data and it'll come up with the right answer.'

'I just would not know what to ask it, Earth; these boys haven't given me a lead. I called to tell you I'm going to throw up the game. They're too powerful! I'm just going to put them the old preservation plea: that every race is unique and should be spared on that account, just as we guard wild animals from extinction in parks – even the dangerous ones. OK?'

The reply came faintly back: *'You're on the spot, feller; we stand by your evaluation. Good luck and out.'*

Stevens looked round at the expressionless faces. Many of the beings present had gigantic ears; one of them possibly – probably – had heard the brief exchange. At that he made his own face expressionless and spoke aloud.

'I have nothing more to say to you,' he announced. 'Indeed, I already wish I had said nothing at all. This court is a farce. If you tried all the insects, would they have a word to say in their defence? No! So you would kill them – and as a result you yourself would die. Insects are a vital factor. So is Man. How can we know our own potentialities? If you know yours, it is because you have ceased to develop and are already doomed to extinction. I demand that Man, who has seen through this *stunt*, be left to develop in his own fashion, unmolested.

'Gentlemen, take me back home!'

He ended in a shout, and carried away by his own outburst expected a round of applause. The silence was broken only by a polite rustling. For a moment, he thought Mordregon glanced encouragingly at him, and then the figures faded away, and he was left standing alone, gesticulating in an empty hall.

A robot came and led him back to the automatic ship.

In what was estimated to be a month, Stevens arrived back at Luna One and was greeted there by Lord Sylvester as he stepped from the galactic vessel.

They pumped each other heartily on the back.

'It worked! I swear it worked!' Stevens told the older man.

'Did you try them with reasoning?' Sylvester asked eagerly.

'Yes – at least, I did my best. But I didn't seem to be getting anywhere, and then I chucked it up. I remembered what you said, that if they were masters of the galaxy they must be practical men to stay there, and that if we dangled before their variegated noses a practical dinkum which they hadn't got they'd be queuing up for it.'

'And they hadn't got an instantaneous communicator!' Sylvester exclaimed, bursting into a hoot of laughter.

'Naturally not, the thing being an impossibility, as our scientists proved long ago! But the funny bit was, Syl, they accidentally *told* me they hadn't got one. *And* I didn't even have to employ that argument for having no mind-readers present.'

'So that little bit of recording we fixed up behind your ugly great ear did the trick?'

'It sounded so absolutely genuine I almost believed it was

the real thing,' Stevens said enthusiastically. 'I'm convinced we've won the day with that gadget.'

And then, perversely, the sense of triumph that had buoyed him all the way home deserted him. The trick was no longer clever; to have duped the Ultralords gave him suddenly nothing but disappointment. With listless surprise at this reaction, he realized he knew himself less well than he had believed.

He glanced at the gibbous Earth, low over Luna's mountains: it was the colour of verdigris.

All the while, Sylvester chattered on excitedly.

'Fine! You knock at least nine years off the ten I've aged since you left! When do we get the verdict, Dave? – the mighty Yea or Nay!'

'Any time now – but I'm convinced the Ultralords are in the bag. Some of the mammoth ears present must have picked your voice up.'

Sylvester commenced to beat Stevens's back again. Then he sobered and said: 'Now we'll have to think about stalling them when they come and ask for portable sub-radios. Still, that can wait; after all, we didn't actually tell them we had them! Meanwhile, I've been stalling off the news-hounds here – the Galactics can't prove more awkward than they've been. Then the President wants to see you – but before that there's a drink waiting for you, and Edwina is sitting nursing it.'

'Lead the way!' Stevens said, a little more happily.

'You look a bit gloomy all of a sudden,' Sylvester commented. 'Tired, I expect?'

'It has been a strain . . .'

As he spoke, the door of his transport slammed shut behind him and the craft lifted purposefully off the field, silent on its cosmic drive. Stevens waved it a solemn farewell and turned away quickly, hurrying with Sylvester across to the domes of Luna One. A chilliness was creeping over him again.

Our Council of the Ultralords must be certain it pronounces the correct verdict when aliens such as Stevens are under examination; consequently, it has to have telepaths present during the trials. All it asks is, simply, integrity in the defendants – that is the simple touchstone: yet it is too difficult for many of them. The men of Earth tortured themselves chasing phantoms, cooking up chimeras. Stevens had integrity, yet would not trust to it. Those who are convicted of dishonesty perish; we have no room for them.

The robot craft swung away from Luna and headed at full speed towards Earth, the motors in its warhead ticking expectantly, counting out the seconds to annihilation.

And that, of course, would be the end of the story – for Earth at least. It would have been completely destroyed, as is usual in such distressing cases, but Mordregon, who was amused by Stevens's bluff, decided that, after all, the warped brains of Earthmen might be useful in coping with the warped brains of the enemy Eleventh Galaxy. He called it 'an expedient war-time measure'.

Quietly, he deflected the speeding missile from its target, ordering it to return home. He sent this message by sub-radio, of course; dangerous aliens must necessarily be deluded at times.

TIME

Not for an Age

He was not for an age, but for all time – *Ben Jonson.*

A bed spring groaned and pinged, mists cleared, Rodney Furnell awoke. From the bathroom next door came the crisp sound of shaving: his son was up. The bed next to his was empty: Valerie, his second wife, was up. Guiltily, Rodney also rose, and performéd several timid exercises to flex his backbone. Youth! When it was going it had to be husbanded. He touched his toes.

The audience had its first laugh there.

By the time Rodney had got into his Sunday suit, Valerie's cuckoo clock was chuckling nine, followed by the more sardonic notes of his ormolu chimer. Valerie and Jim (Rodney had conscientiously shunned a literary name for his only offspring) were already at the cornflakes when he entered their gay little kitchenette.

More laughter at the first sight of that antiquated twentieth-century modernity.

'Hello, both! Lovely morning,' he boomed, kissing Valerie's forehead. The September sun, in fact, was making a fair showing through damp mist: a man of forty-two instinctively arms himself with enthusiasm when facing a wife fifteen years younger.

The audience always loved the day's meals, murmuring with delight as each quaint accessory – toaster, teapot, sugar tongs – was used.

Valerie looked fresh and immaculate. Jim sported an open-necked shirt and was attentive to his step-mother. At nineteen, he was too manly, and too attentive . . . He shared the Sunday paper companionably with her, chatting about the theatre and books. Sometimes Rodney could join in about one of the books. Under the notion that Valerie disliked seeing him in spectacles, he refrained from reading at breakfast.

How the audience roared later when he slipped them on in his study! How he hated that audience! How fervently he wished that he had the power to raise even one eyebrow in scorn of them!

The day wore on exactly as it had done for over a thousand times, unable to deviate in the slightest from its original course. So it would go on and on, as meaningless as a cliché, or a tune endlessly repeated: for the benefit of these fools who stood on all four sides and laughed at the silliest things.

At first, Rodney had been frightened. This power to snatch them all as it were from the grave had seemed something occult. Then, becoming accustomed to it, he had been flattered. That these wise beings had wanted to review *his* day, disinter *his* modest life ... it was balm only for a time, Rodney soon discovered he was only a glorified side-show at some latter-day fair, a butt for fools and not an edification for philosophers.

He walked in the tumble-down garden with Valerie, his arm round her waist. The North Oxford air was mild and sleepy, the neighbours' radio was off.

'Have you *got* to go and see that desiccated old Regius Professor, darling?' she asked.

'You know I must.' He conquered his irritation and added— 'We'll go for a drive after lunch – just you and I.'

Unfailingly, each day's audience laughed at that. Presumably 'a drive after lunch' had come to mean something dubious in their day. Each time Rodney made that remark, he dreaded the reaction from those half-glimpsed countenances that pressed on all sides: yet he was powerless to alter what had once been said.

He kissed Valerie, he hoped elegantly, the audience tittered, and he stepped into the garage. His wife returned to the house, and Jim. What happened in there he would never know, however many times the day was repeated. There was no way of confirming his suspicion that his son was in love with Valerie and she attracted to him. She should have enough sense to prefer a mature man to a stripling of nineteen: besides, it was only eighteen months since he had been referred to in print as 'one of our promising young men of litterae historicae'.

Rodney could have walked round to Septuagint College. But because the car was new and something that his don's salary would hardly stretch to, he preferred to drive. The watchers, of course, shrieked with laughter at the sight of his little Morris ten. He occupied himself, as he polished the windscreen, with hating the audience and all inhabitants of this future world.

That was the strange thing. There was room in the corner of the old Rodney's mind for the new Rodney's ghost. He depended on the old Rodney – the Rodney who had actually lived that fine, autumn day – for vision, motion, all the paraphernalia of life, but he could occupy independently a tiny cell of his consciousness. He was a helpless observer carried over and over in a cockpit of the past.

The irony of it lay there. He would have been spared all this humiliation if he did not know what was happening. But he did know, trapped though he was in an unknowing shell.

Even to Rodney, a history man and no scientist, the broad outline of what had happened was obvious enough. Somewhen in the future, man had ferreted out the secret of literally reclaiming the past. Bygone years lay in the rack of antiquity like film spools in a library. Like film spools, they were not amenable to change, but might be played over and over on a suitable projector. Rodney's autumn day was being played over and over.

He had reflected helplessly on the situation so often that the horror of it had worn thin. That day had passed, quietly, trivially, had been forgotten; suddenly long afterwards, it had been whipped back among the things that were. Its actions, even its thoughts, had been reconstituted, with only Rodney's innermost ego to suffer from the imposition. How unsuspecting he had been then! How inadequate every one of his gestures seemed now, performed twice, ten, a hundred, a thousand times!

Had he been as smug every day as he was that day? And what had happened after that day? Having, naturally, no knowledge of the rest of his life then, he had none now. If he had been happy with Valerie for much longer, if his recently published work on feudal justice had been acclaimed, were questions he could pose without answering.

A pair of Valerie's gloves lay on the back seat of the car; Rodney threw them into a locker with an éclat quite

73

divorced from his inner impotence. She, poor dear bright thing, was in the same predicament. In that they were united, although powerless to express the union by any slightest flicker of expression.

He drove slowly down Banbury Road. As ever, there were four sub-divisions of reality. There was the external world of Oxford; there were Rodney's original abstracted observations as he moved through the world; there were the ghost thoughts of the 'present-I', bitter and frustrated; there were the half-seen faces of the future which advanced or receded aimlessly. The four blended indefinably, one becoming another in Rodney's moments of near madness. (What would it be like to be insane, trapped in a sane mind? He was tempted by the luxury of letting go.)

Sometimes he caught snatches of talk from the onlookers. They at least varied from day to day. 'If he knew what he looked like!' they would exclaim. Or: 'Do you see her hair-do?' Or: 'Can you beat that for a slum!' Or: 'Mummy, what's that funny brown thing he's eating?' Or – how often he heard that one: 'I just wish he knew we were watching him!'

Church bells were solemnly ringing as he pulled up outside Septuagint and switched off the ignition. Soon he would be in that fusty study, taking a glass of something with the creaking old Regius Professor. For the nth time he would be smiling a shade too much as the grip of ambition outreached the hand of friendship. His mind leapt ahead and back and ahead and back again in a frenzy. Oh, if he could only *do* something! So the day would pass. Finally, the night would come – one last gust of derision at Valerie's nightdress and his pyjamas! – and then oblivion.

Oblivion ... that lasted an eternity but took no time at all ... And *they* wound the reel back and started it again, all over again.

He was pleased to see the Regius Professor. The Regius Professor was pleased to see him. Yes, it was a nice day. No, he hadn't been out of college since, let's see, it must be the summer before last. And then came that line that drew the biggest laugh of all; Rodney said, inevitably: 'Oh, we must all hope for some sort of immortality.'

To have to say it again, to have to say it not a shade less glibly than when it had first been said, and when the wish had been granted already in such a ludicrous fashion! If only he might die first, if only the film would break down!

And then the film did break down.

The universe flickered to a standstill and faded into dim purple. Temperature and sound slid down to zero. Rodney Furnell stood transfixed, his arms extended in the middle of a gesture, a wineglass in his right hand. The flicker, the purple, the zeroness cut down through him; but even as he sensed himself beginning to fade, a great fierce hope was born within him. With a burst of avidity, the ghost of him took over the old Rodney. Confidence flooded him as he fought back the negativity.

The wineglass vanished from his hand. The Regius Professor sank into twilight and was gone. Blackness reigned. Rodney turned round. It was a voluntary movement: *it was not in the script:* he was alive, free.

The bubble of twentieth-century time had burst, leaving him alive in the future. He stood in the middle of a black and barren area. There had evidently been a slight explosion. Overhead was a crane-like affair as big as a locomotive with several funnels protruding from its underside; smoke issued from one of the funnels. Doubtless the thing was a time-projector or whatever it might be called, and obviously it had blown a valve.

The scene about him engaged all Rodney's attention. He was delighted to see that his late audience had been thrown into mild panic by the sudden collapse of the chimera. They shouted and pushed and – in one quarter – fought vigorously. Male and female alike, they wore featureless, transparent bags which encased them from neck to ankle: and they had had the impertinence to laugh at his pyjamas!

Cautiously, Rodney moved away. At first, the idea of liberty overwhelmed him, he could scarcely believe himself alive. Then the realization came: his liberty was precious – how doubly precious after that most terrible form of captivity! – and he must guard it by flight. He hurried beyond the projection area, pausing at a great sign that read:

75

CHRONOARCHAEOLOGY LTD PRESENTS –
THE SIGHTS OF THE CENTURIES
COME AND ENJOY THE ANTICS OF YOUR
ANCESTORS!
YOU'LL LAUGH AS YOU LEARN

And underneath: Please Take One.

Shaking, Rodney seized a gaudy folder and stuffed it into his pocket. Then he ran.

His guess about the fair-ground was correct, and Valerie and he had been merely a glorified 'What the Butler Saw'. Gigantic booths towered on all sides. Gay crowds sauntered or stood, taking little notice as Rodney passed. Flags flew, silvery music sounded; nearby, a flashing sign begged:

TRY ANTI-GRAV AND REALIZE YOUR DREAMS

further, a banner proclaimed:

THE SINISTER VENUSIANS ARE *HERE*!

Fortunately, a gateway was close. Dreading a detaining hand on his arm, Rodney made for it as quickly as possible. He passed a towering structure before which a queue of people gazed lasciviously up at the word:

SAVOUR THE EROTIC POSSIBILITIES OF
FREE-FALL

and came to the entrance.

An attendant called 'Hi!' and made to stop him. Rodney broke into a run. He ran down a satin-smooth road until exhaustion overcame him. A metal object shaped vaguely like a shoe but as big as a small bungalow stood in the kerb. Through its windows, Rodney saw couches and no human beings. Thankful at the mute offer of rest and concealment, he climbed in.

As he sank panting on to yielding rubber-foam, he realized what a horrible situation he was in. To be stranded centuries ahead of his own lifetime – and death – in a world of supertechnology and barbarism! – For so he visualized it. However, it was a vast improvement on the repetitive nightmare he had recently endured. Chiefly, now, he needed time to think quietly.

'Are you ready to proceed, sir?'

Rodney jumped up, startled by a voice so near him. Nobody was in sight. The interior resembled a coach's, with wide soft seats, all of which were empty.

'Are you ready to proceed, sir?' There it was again.

'Who is that?' Rodney asked.

'This is Auto-moto Seven Six One Mu at your service, sir, awaiting instructions to proceed.'

'You mean away from here?'

'Certainly, sir.'

'Yes, please!'

At once the structure was gliding smoothly forward. No noise, no vibration. The gaudy fair-ground fell back and was replaced by other buildings, widely spaced, smokeless, mainly built of a substance which looked like curtain fabric; they flowed by without end.

'Are you – are we heading for the country?' Rodney asked.

'This is the country, sir. Do you require a city?'

'No, I don't. What is there beside city and country?'

'Nothing, sir – except of course the sea fields.'

Dropping that line of questioning, Rodney, who was instinctively addressing a busy control board at the front of the vehicle, inquired: 'Excuse my asking, but are you a – er, robot?'

'Yes, sir. Auto-moto Seven Six One Mu. New on this route, sir.'

Rodney breathed a sigh of relief. He could not have faced a human being but irrationally felt superior to a mere mechanical. Pleasant voice it had, no more grating certainly than the Professor of Anglo-Saxon at his old college . . . however long ago that was.

'What year *is* this?' he asked.

'Circuit Zero, Epoch Eighty Two, new style. Year Two Thousand Five Hundred Anno Domini, old style.'

It was the first direct confirmation of all his suspicions: there was no gainsaying that level voice.

'Thanks,' he said hollowly. 'Now if you don't mind I've got to think.'

Thought, however, yielded little in comfort or results. Possibly the wisest course would be to throw himself at the mercy of some civilized authority – if there were any civilized authorities left. And would the wisest course in a twentieth-century world be the wisest in a – um, twenty-six-century world?

'Driver, is Oxford in existence?'

'What is Oxford, sir?'

A twinge of anxiety as he asked: 'This is England?'

'Yes, sir. I have found Oxford in my directory, sir. It is a motor and space-ship factory in the Midlands, sir.'

'Just keep going.'

Dipping into his pocket, he produced the fun-fair brochure and scanned its bright lettering, hoping for a clue to action.

'Chronarchaeology Ltd present a staggering series of Peeps into the Past. Whole days in the lives of (a) A Mother Dinosaur, (b) William the Conqueror's Wicked Nephew, (c) A Citizen of Crazed, Plague-Ridden Stuart London, (d) A Twentieth-Century Teacher in Love.

'Nothing expurgated, nothing added! Better than the Feelies! All in glorious 4D – no stereos required.'

Fuming at the description of himself, Rodney crumpled the brochure in his hand. He wondered bitterly how many of his own generation were helplessly enduring this gross irreverence in peepshows all over the world. When the sense of outrage abated slightly, curiosity reasserted itself; he smoothed out the folder and read a brief description of the process which 'will give you history-sterics as it brings each era nearer'.

Below the heading 'It's Fabulous – It's Pabulous!' he read, 'Just as anti-gravity lifts a man against the direction of weight, chrono-grab can lift a machine out of the direction of time and send it speeding back over the dark centuries. It can be accurately guided from the present to scoop up a fragment from the past, slapping that fragment – all unknown to the people in it – right into your lucky laps. The terrific expense of this intricate operation need hardly be emphas—'

'Driver!' Rodney screamed. 'Do you know anything about this time-grabbing business?'

'Only what I have heard, sir.'

'What do you mean by that?'

'My built-in information centre contains only facts relating to my duty, sir, but since I also have learning circuits I am occasionally able to collect gossip from passengers which—'

'Tell me this, then: can human beings as well as machines travel back in time?'

The buildings were still flashing by, silent, hostile in the unknown world. Drumming his fingers wildly on his seat, Rodney awaited an answer.

'Only machines, sir. Humans can't live backwards.'

For a long time he lay and cried comfortably. The auto-moto made solacing cluck-cluck noises, but it was a situation with which it was incompetent to deal.

At last, Rodney wiped his eyes on his sleeve, the sleeve of his Sunday suit, and sat up. He directed the driver to head for the main offices of Chronoarchaeology and slumped back in a kind of stupor. Only at the headquarters of that fiendish invention might there be people who could – if they would – restore him to his own time.

Rodney dreaded the thought of facing any creature of this unscrupulous age. He pressed the idea away, and concentrated instead on the peace and orderliness of the world from which he had been resurrected. To see Oxford again, to see Valerie . . . Dear, dear Valerie.

Would they help him at Chronoarchaeology? Or – *supposing the people at the fair-ground repaired their devilish apparatus before he got there* . . . What would happen then he shuddered to imagine.

'Faster, driver,' he shouted.

The wide-spaced buildings became a wall.

'Faster, driver,' he screamed.

The wall became a mist.

'We are doing mach 2·3, sir,' said the driver calmly.

'Faster!'

The mist became a scream.

'We are about to crash, sir.'

They crashed. Blackness, merciful, complete.

A bed spring groaned and pinged and the mists cleared. Rodney awoke. From the bathroom next door came the crisp, repetitive sound of Jim shaving.

The Shubshub Race

The clock tower of the palace of Harkon looked out over the chill sea.

King Able Harkon Horace sat in a small room of the palace, also gazing out at the meaningless expanse of water. He failed to guess what a momentous day this was to be; his preoccupation, as usual, was with his illness.

Although only in his mid-thirties, the king's face was already lined with suffering, and his eyes burned with the febrile brightness of an overburdened brain. No man could diagnose what ailed him; hundreds had tried or pretended to try. Nothing could ward off those terrible periods when, for days on end, he fell into a swoon and lay rigidly on his bed, groaning that time had stopped and the world was ending.

King Horace ruled a small Earth kingdom on the edge of the North Sea, one of those quiet kingdoms which sprang up after the establishment of the zero-zero space drive and the collapse of World Government. Its chief industries were fishing and the manufacture of sand-glazed chaperchers for the control templates of spaceship boosters.

With a nervous movement, the king rose from his throne.

'Silence!' he said irritably, for it had been reading to him. He was restless, thinking of his visit to the health planet Upotia. Tomorrow he would start on his way to that happy world – for in those times, as now, Upotia was famed throughout the galaxy for its blessedly stable climates, although nowadays it is becoming a little overcrowded.

Making a gesture of impatience, he stalked out on to the promenade with the aid of his stick. Sweeping the view with a sick and listless gaze, he observed approaching the palace his Air Vice-Marshal: for in this kingdom, vice was not allowed on the ground.

The Air Vice-Marshal was leading by the collar a handsome man in a white uniform with rather too natty brown gloves, who walked along protesting loudly that it was a free country.

'Who's that fellow?' King Horace asked, pointing at the white uniform with his stick: 'Never seen him before.'

The AVM, bowing low, begged His Majesty not to be deceived by the other's haughty airs: he was only a common wrongdoer named Swap who had just been caught with a girl committing vice in the palace grounds. He was to be executed tomorrow.

'Good,' said the king.

'—!' said the captive, and was at once hauled away.

Increasingly restless now, the king made off by the side gate and went down a shingly twisting lane to the margins of the grey sea. The wind blew no warmer for its being May, and he pulled his cloak more tightly about him. God, but he was sick of everything, his own disease as much as others' health. That fellow Swat . . . no, Swap . . .

A voice at his elbow, in a tone that admitted no doubt, said: 'I know your cure.'

King Horace perceived he was being addressed by a chunky figure five feet high who wore a strange habit and kept his face concealed. The king's anger was at once aroused, but there were no guards within call, and to his questions the creature gave no reply except to say that he was an oracle who had travelled many light years to sell the king something: the key to his health.

'You are singularly rude for a tradesman,' exclaimed the king.

The oracle spat.

'Diagnose me,' demanded the king, shaking with irritation and expectation together. The oracle for answer produced from his habit a wafer-thin circle of metal as large as a plate, which he pronounced to contain the key to King Horace's suffering. Eagerly, the king stretched out a hand for it.

'Money first,' snapped the oracle. 'I must have payment or you will have no confidence in the cure.'

'You'll have to come to the palace then, I've no money on me.'

'You think me a fool? To be locked in one of your insanitary dungeons? Give me your stick – that'll be payment enough.'

Now the king's stick was indeed valuable. It contained, besides the usual umbrella, dagger and stun-gun, phials of curative powders, with cyanide and elastoplast for emergencies, a small stock of gold, a miniature 3D of Betsy Gorble, telestar, and a mind-defacer which automatically blanketed the bearer's neural projections, if any esp-men were in the neighbourhood. The stick, therefore, was a treasure; nevertheless, King Horace exchanged it after only momentary hesitation for the metal plate. At once the oracle padded behind a sand-dune and was gone.

As if paralysed, the king stared down at his acquisition. A gust of wind whipped it from his palm and blew it towards the sea. With a cry, the king ran after it over the wet sand. Two floating gulls rose shrieking from the waves and wheeled over him. Lines of foam lapped round the plate, dragging it back with their retreat. He pounced on it; it eluded him. Then, stretching forward desperately, he seized it.

He stepped back, spray bursting over his cloak – and trod on nothing!

In a flash, he was up to his thighs in quicksand. Only the bottomless muds of Earth lay below him. Instinctively he threw himself flat, clawing with frantic hands to reach solidity and safety. The sea pounded and the gulls screamed and his heart drummed. Inch by inch, he tore himself out of the coldly sucking filth. He lay then for an hour, sobbing and resting, before growing strong enough to crawl back to the palace.

When his servants and physicians had bathed, reproached and given him sedatives, King Horace had a rare flash of gratitude. His life had been spared: he would spare a life.

'Order that fellow Swap to be pardoned and brought here,' he said, thinking: 'Mine is a poor life, after all, compared with his.'

He lay back amid pillows and a servant appeared with the metal plate, which King Horace had thrust into the bosom of his tunic and forgotten in his struggle with the sands. Dismissing the servant, he held it in shaking hands and then prised it open. A momentary resistance, the hiss of collapsing vacuum and the lid came up. On the bottom plate was a white strip bearing an obscure sentence:

ON GLOBADAN I WON THE SHUBSHUB RACE

King Horace's face twisted bitterly. He stabbed at the message to pluck it away, but it formed part of the plate. Tears burned in his eyes: how could that nonsense cure him? Even as he peered at it again, the wording writhed and faded till not a trace remained. He stared for a moment more, then sent the plate scudding far out of the palace window.

Next morning, King Horace was in poor shape. He appeared obsessed with the idea of leaving for Upotia, sick as he was: nobody could dissuade him. Swap arrived and was ordered to escort the king on pain of having his sentence reimposed. They made for the tiny space port, the king ignoring the glad farewells of his subjects. Once there, he dismissed his courtiers with a glum wave of the hand, and hobbled into the lift of SS *Potent*. In a moment more he was whisked up out of sight. Swap, two elderly nurses and a baggage man followed without enthusiasm; they formed all his retinue.

Spaceships, it is frequently said, are inventions of the devil. But in King Horace's day the devil was obviously less of an engineer than he is now. The ship which bore the king – not, incidentally, one of his own, for his kingdom was too small to finance more than moon freighters – belonged to the Solar-(Upotia-Vegan and All Stations for Andromeda) Line and was a tub. To be more precise, it was cramped, had a poor *cuisine* and boasted almost no turn of speed. So the unpleasant journey was also protracted, the seven light years taking nearly four weeks to cover.

Nevertheless, Upotia was worth a little discomfort.

For the early part of the journey, the king preserved a reflective silence. He brooded chiefly on the question of the oracle, for although his message had been, at best, a conundrum, the man himself was as much of a riddle. Was he genuine or a trickster? The odds seemed evenly balanced. On the one hand, his complete indifference to the person of the king argued a certain authority noticeably lacking in all the quacks who had previously presented their fawning selves at court; on the other hand, if he had anything of real value to offer, it seemed likely he would have insisted on greater reward than he had, in fact, received – his passage paid home, at the least.

Now he had vanished, leaving only a sentence of uncertain meaning.

King Horace was still undecided when they touched lightly down on Upotia.

Most planets, like Earth itself, provide all sorts of weather, although a few like Venus possess only bad: but Upotia enjoys only good. This is due partly to an exceptionally deep atmosphere, partly to its axial inclination and partly to the multiple sun system of which it is the only habitable planet.

'Delightful!' exclaimed the king, inhaling deeply.

'Absolutely!' echoed Swap. His first surliness had long since faded. Once he fully realized what an easy number he had fallen into, he was as agreeable as it was in his uncertain nature to be. The voyage had forced him into the king's company: they were much of an age: when allowances were made for the king's infirmity he was not such a bad chap: he had given Swap the Royal Pardon: they were going on holiday – and the King had told him about the oracle and 'On Globadan I won the Shubshub race'.

'At least we know what shubshubs are,' said Swap, as who should say: '—and a fat lot of good that does us!'

'Do you?' said the king eagerly. 'I don't! I thought it was a bit of gibberish. What are shubshubs? Sweets?'

'Of course you've led a very secluded life,' said Swap, mastering the big word with difficulty. And he explained that shubshubs were rare and expensive animals like six-legged ostriches which ran more swiftly than leopards. Where they came from he did not know, nor had he ever seen one.

Perhaps there *was* something in the message after all. Hope began to circulate again in the king's blood; after all, surely if the oracle had been a fraud he would have taken care to be more ingratiating?

'We may find out more about this on Upotia,' the king said.

But they found out no more on Upotia. For one thing, there was a deal of snobbery among the rich invalids there, and those who had seen the king land not in his private craft but in a common liner cut him dead. So the king and Swap (and the two elderly nurses) roamed the country by caracar, away from the centres of population.

They had been there a fortnight of golden days when they met the Priestess Colinette Shawl. King Horace had by now grown tired of Swap and the limitations of his mind: for though at first he had been titillated by the other's accounts of romantic wrong-doing back in the palace grounds, he soon wearied of what sounded rather an empty routine. Accordingly, he was more ready to welcome the priestess.

'This is my entourage,' he said, reluctantly introducing Swap.

'Charmed,' they said together, and Swap rested thoughtful and commanding eyes on the newcomer – for where the priestess came from priestesses were picked for their power to attract the parishioners. That indeed was her business on Upotia: to make converts to her sect. She began straightaway on the king and Swap, and when it grew dark she pitched her tent beside theirs.

After midnight the third and fourth suns rose. The fourth was a glinting speck hundreds of millions of miles away, while the third was a dull, fuzzy giant, trailing over the horizon like a shock of red hair. Together they made little more light than Luna, but the effect was very romantic.

Possibly you recall the old saying about the chlorophyll being greener in someone else's grass. Swap also recalled it as he lay and meditated on the discomfort of his bed; he was unable to sleep.

At last he rose, and padded out to Priestess Colinette's tent. He knocked gently on the wooden door-pole.

'I'm converted!' he whispered.

The priestess, who had heard that one before, came circumspectly forth and delivered a religious address.

'What is more,' she added, 'it is too late to start anything. Tomorrow I begin the voyage back to Globadan.'

'Globadan!' shouted Swap. 'You mean to say you come from Globadan? There is such a dump! Hey, skipper – wake up!'

And he pulled the king out of bed, much to the latter's displeasure. Swap had acted with his usual thoughtlessness.

Nevertheless, hope that the oracle's message might after all bear some significance silenced the royal irritation, and in none too horrible a voice the king told Priestess Shawl the whole business, hoping she might throw more light upon it.

' "On Globadan I won the shubshub race",' she echoed. 'Unless that was written by another shubshub, it's pure nonsense. *Nothing*, absolutely nothing on legs can beat a shubshub.'

'OK. It's nonsense. Let's go back to bed!' said Swap, suddenly tiring of the whole thing. 'It would be me have to go getting tied up with neurotic kings . . .' he reflected.

'You go,' said the king. 'I want to ask the priestess a couple of questions—'

('I'll wait till *you* go,' said Swap; he wasn't born yesterday.)

'—are these shubshub races an institution on Globadan?'

The priestess said they were staged every year.

'May anything but a shubshub enter for them?'

A study of criminal punishment throughout the galaxy yields much interest. On Globadan, according to the priestess, it was the tradition to release certain more harmless criminals and let them enter for the shubshub races with the promise of liberty if they won. Some tried hard and died of heart-failure on the course. This custom added a spice of humour to the day's events.

'Has any human ever won?' pressed the king.

'As I said, it would be impossible,' said the priestess, adding somewhat illogically: 'Certainly nobody did it in my time. But you must remember that Globadan is out on the rim of the galaxy, and I have been away on missionary work since I was virtually a child. Can't you imagine just how excited I am to think I'm on my way back there tomorrow?'

'But nobody *could* beat a shubshub,' pressed the king.

'*Nobody* could beat a shubshub,' agreed the priestess.

'Nobody could beat a *shubshub*,' Swap told them.

They had it straight. All three returned to their separate beds. King Horace spent a restless night, Swap slept deeply, Priestess Shawl was gone by morning.

The malady which was never far from the king returned that day and laid him low. He lay and sweated with a body